# Multiple Myeloma – The Race to Find A Cure

## A Runner's Memoir

**Second Edition**

**By Paul Chenery**

大難不死，必有後福

"If you can survive a big disaster, luck will follow you the rest of your life."

- Chinese Proverb

To my wife Felomina

For her strength, courage and determination

And for crossing the finish line with me each and every day


To Tita Mila

For her unconditional support to our family

Right from the day we first met up to the present

# Foreword

My name is Dr. Serge Capacete, Head of Space Medicine at the One-System Integrated Health Network in Boston, Massachusetts. I discovered this book in our National Holographic Archives Library in the year 2096. It was collecting dust in the ancient hard-cover written editions section. As far as I know, it is the only surviving copy which was written by Paul Chenery in the year 2021.

I came across it quite by accident while searching for a book on marathon training. I noticed that the book was lacking a 'Foreword' section. I took the liberty of writing this section and then sending it back in time through the quantum space-time portal for inclusion in the book. Perhaps Mr. Chenery did not realize that this part of a book is important and usually produced by an independent expert authority in an effort to lend credibility to the book. Or perhaps he could not find a suitable author willing to make a contribution.

I found the book to be extremely compelling, not for the running advice offered within its pages, but for the final chapter that predicted the cure for multiple myeloma. Amazingly, the science behind the prediction is 99% accurate. There is no evidence that Chenery possesses any medical credentials. I can only assume that Mr. Chenery secretly discovered the quantum space-time portal and then 'stole the future research' that resulted in the cure. What a clever rascal! If only I could travel back to 2021 and shake his hand, or at least give him a post-COVID-19 elbow bump! Unfortunately, living organisms cannot survive travel via the portal, only inanimate objects such as this piece that I am currently writing.

For Mr. Chenery's insights, I plan to nominate him posthumously for an honorary medical degree. The book will also be submitted for consideration of a Nobel prize in literature, although it is very rare for a non-fiction book to be awarded this distinction.

The book is an intriguing mix of history, science, fiction and a deeply moving personal journey as a patient caregiver and advocate for his wife Mina, who survived three different cancers, including multiple myeloma. Although this disease is non-existent in my lifetime, we can learn much from the lessons of our past.

Next Monday is Patriots Day in Massachusetts and I am registered to run in the 200th anniversary of the Boston Marathon. I note that Mr. Chenery's best performance in that historic race was 3:01. He ran the 100th anniversary edition of the race back in 1996. He also became the oldest Boston Marathon finisher at the age of 89 in the year 2045. During his running career, Paul also became an accomplished ultra-marathoner. I am unsure if I can match Paul's running performances, but I plan to put in my best effort.

As I compose this, the future is experiencing the possibility of an interplandemic, which is a new term coined to describe a pandemic that spreads between two worlds. The colonization of Mars, which began in the 2030s, has turned into an unmitigated disaster. After several colonies were established on the Martian planet, an aggressive alien microbe began to infect the population on the planet. This resulted in accelerated non-abiogenesis evolution, where the DNA of the human settlers began to mutate instantly. The result is an entirely separate species which is hostile to humankind and much more advanced in terms of intelligence. I implore the scientists of the past who developed the Mars colonization program not to proceed. Consider instead a colonization program for Titan, Saturn's largest moon.

It is amazing. As I finish this section of the book and send it backwards in time, it is appearing before me in the future. Enjoy Paul's story of multiple myeloma. It will inspire you.

Dr. Serge Capacete, M.D.
One-System Integrated Health Network
Boston, Massachusetts
April, 2096

# Preface

The title of this book may be an enigma to anyone who casually glimpses the cover. What relationship does multiple myeloma have with running? More importantly, what benefit will a multiple myeloma patient and their caregiver derive from reading this material, which is written from the perspective of an experienced marathon and ultra-marathon runner? Beyond the obvious connection between a healthy lifestyle activity and disease prevention, the link between the two is more nuanced than one would expect.

This book is written as a dedication to my wife, Felomina (Mina), a multiple myeloma patient, who was diagnosed with the disease in April of 2019. She is also a survivor of thyroid cancer (2001) and oral cancer (2018). The book is a collection of our anecdotal experiences and personal interactions as we ran the multiple myeloma race together. There is a bit of medical jargon mainly related to Mina's cancer tests which I have included for context. I have attempted to keep this to a minimum since there are plenty of other books written by doctors and researchers who are the appropriate subject matter experts in this area.

I wanted to write a book about multiple myeloma that would not only capture Mina's experience but would also serve as an inspirational story and a guide to other myeloma patients and caregivers. Multiple myeloma is a complex disease with its own complex language, couched in medical terminology that is enough to make a layperson's head spin. I am not a medical doctor and had zero knowledge of blood cancers prior to learning of my wife's diagnosis.

Knowing that 'knowledge is power', I was desperate to find answers to arm myself with information that would allow me to have an intelligent understanding of this disease. This would enable me to be the best patient advocate and caregiver on the planet. One does not need to attend medical school to achieve this lofty goal, however, one needs to invest time, energy and effort in a little bit of research in order to translate medical-speak into plain English (or whatever your first language might be).

You also need to have a system in place to monitor and track progress over the course of treatment. There is a requirement to understand the roles and responsibilities of the various medical specialists, who are all part of the team. They are all standing at the myeloma race start line with you. Your task is to 'get up to speed with them' to ensure you do not get left behind before you cross the start line. There is also a need to recruit friends and family as another pillar of support and become your own personal cheerleaders as you race towards the finish line. Many times, the task seemed impossible and it felt like I was running uphill in a never-ending marathon, begging for the finish line to come into sight. Runners often 'hit the wall' at the twenty-mile point of a 26.2-mile marathon. As I conducted my own research into multiple myeloma, it was like hitting several walls. Medicine is a science, however, as a layman, I came to discover through my caregiver role that there is a science to understanding medicine.

The internet became my go-to research tool. Fortunately, many years ago, I had taken the Psychology Specialist Program at the University of Toronto. I never imagined that I would be using the research tools from Psychology in a practical real-world sense. I had written academic papers that followed the structure of the scientific method. I understood the concepts of randomized control groups, probability testing and the importance of peer reviewed research. But this can only take you so far. The research papers posted to the internet were filled with complex language that I had to weed through. To add insult to injury, the science behind multiple myeloma was changing as rapidly as an elite Kenyan marathoner's pace.

I also benefited from my Bachelor of Commerce degree from Carleton University in Ottawa. I had spent most of my career as a specialist in financial planning and budgeting. We finance professionals love to deal with numbers, analyze trends and write copious amounts of detail into monthly reports. Keeping a daily diary of Mina's treatment and results was therefore no big deal for me. I recorded everything that I thought would be relevant to my role.

I borrowed this concept from my experience as a runner over the past twenty-six years. Runners incorporate a daily training log into their routine that captures key elements of their training program. Everything from the number of kilometres run to the daily weather conditions gets written down. This obsession with detailed record-keeping later proved to be invaluable, especially with our interactions with doctors, pharmacists, cardiologists, nephrologists, hepatologists, radiologists and dentists.

Since running, and not medical science, is a language that I am intimately familiar with, I developed the idea for this book with the intent of using running metaphors to help you, the reader, navigate the path towards the myeloma race finish line. My wife and I began this race together, as a team. I assumed the role of her own personal 'pacer.' Despite numerous potholes and speed bumps encountered on course, we are still running together strongly, ever hopeful that the finish line cure is just around the next corner or perhaps over that gigantic clinical trial hill ahead.

My second hobby, other than running, is second language acquisition, specifically Chinese Mandarin. This book contains references to a selection of ancient Chinese idioms, mainly to help inject a feeling of inspiration and hope within the reader. Language is not simply a collection of words strung together within the confines of grammatical rules. It is a complex system of communication with deeply embedded cultural icons and symbolic meanings. In short, foreign language expressions help illuminate our understanding of multiple myeloma by using some universal symbols that we all can easily relate to.

This book is about my experience as a multiple myeloma patient advocate and caregiver. Patient advocacy and caregiving are two distinct roles, but they are not mutually exclusive terms. They are complementary to each other.

The definition of a patient advocate as a person who helps patients communicate with their healthcare providers so they get the information they need to make decisions about their health care. Patient advocates may also help patients set up appointments for doctor visits and medical tests and get financial, legal, and social support. They may also work with insurance companies, employers, case managers, lawyers, and others who may have an impact on a patient's healthcare needs.

The definition of a patient caregiver is a person who gives care to people who need help taking care of themselves. The caregiver is a paid or unpaid and without formal training (in the related treatment) member of a person's social network who helps them with activities of daily living. Caregivers may be health professionals, family members, friends, social workers, or members of the clergy. They may give care at home or in a hospital or other health care setting.

The writing of this book took place during the COVID-19 pandemic. This posed additional challenges both for Mina, the patient, and myself as the patient advocate-caregiver. Mina was in the high-risk category with co-morbidities that included diabetes and high blood pressure. Myeloma conferences and the Toronto Myeloma support group meetings were either deferred or cancelled. Hospital appointments had to be changed to virtual or telephone appointments. For necessary in-person hospital visits, I had to coordinate with hospital administrators in order to get a special visitor's pass to accompany Mina for routine blood tests and to pick up her myeloma maintenance medications from the hospital pharmacy. We had to take extra safety precautions in terms of adhering to physical distancing guidelines, face mask wearing and hand hygiene. Some procedures such as the monthly Zometa (a bone strengthening drug) infusions were deferred, as were the post stem cell transplant vaccinations.

I had previously booked a trip to New York City in October of 2020 to run the Multiple Myeloma Research Foundation's 'Journey Towards A Cure' 12-Hour endurance run. As an ultra-runner, this event was right in my wheelhouse. I was really excited at the prospect of running for twelve hours and raising money for the cause! Of course, we absolutely were not going to travel to the center of the pandemic! Runners may be a little bit crazy, but they are not insane.

The first few sections in this book covering the period from 1844 to 1947 is a mix of historical fact, science, fiction and fantasy. I will let you the reader make the determination as to which elements fall into which category. The tone may appear to be ominous, but the symbolism underlies a prophetic vision of the future that is intended to inspire hope for multiple myeloma patients and caregivers. There are also some lessons we can learn from the darker side of human nature.

The middle chapters document our personal journey through three different cancer diagnoses. You will see running used frequently, both as a metaphor and a promotion of a healthy lifestyle. I also offer my humble advice on how to become the best patient caregiver and advocate by becoming a 'multiple myeloma guru.' Again, there is some medical terminology which could not be avoided. If one is to grasp the true nature of the disease, I would be doing the reader a huge disservice if such material were omitted. However, I have included simplified explanations using plain English where possible.

The final chapter in this book reflects my own optimistic vision of the future. It represents a mix of science, fiction and pure fantasy. If a cure for multiple myeloma appears within the next thirty years, intuitively, it would make sense for an approach that involves the integration of medicine, artificial intelligence (AI), quantum computing, physics and bio-chemistry. I am neither a physicist, doctor or scientist. However, the history of advances in medical technology provides a roadmap of what a possible cure could look like.

Some discoveries happen by accident or through a fortunate coincidence. Many other achievements come about as a result of hard work involving clinical trials and data analysis. The bottom-line is that knowledge builds upon itself. It would not be entirely outside the realm of probability to imagine a convergence of CRISPR, nano-technology and quantum physics to be the catalyst that results in a cure.

We would like to give our sincere thanks to all of the wonderful support received from the Princess Margaret Hospital in Toronto, one of the top cancer research and treatment centres in the world. And our heartfelt thanks are extended to our close family and friends who have given their unconditional support, right from the sound of the starting gun. Whether you are a myeloma patient, caregiver or a serious runner, we hope you all get inspiration and hope from the words written within these pages.

Paul Chenery

February, 2021

# 1844 : Dr. Solly's Folly

Lady Agnes Whipdale sat by her fireplace in her wealthy neighbourhood of Westminster, London. She was counting the day's receipts from her business enterprise located in the notorious slum quarter of St. Giles in Central London. Lady Whipdale ran a simple clothing shop in the upper level of the building. The lower level had a decidedly unique flavour to it. Customers could enter through a secret doorway and proceed stealthily to an extremely more profitable venue called the 'Gentlemen's After-Hours Society.' To Lady Whipdale, the line that separated good and evil or even moral and immoral was a very blurry one indeed. She was proud that she possessed a flexible sense of purpose. The accumulation of wealth has a strange way of shaping one's attitudes.

People had primal needs and desires, with food, shelter and physical release belonging to the top priorities. If she had to put a label on it, she would claim that she was in the business of 'desire fulfilment.' There were two basic groups in 19th century London. Either you were a 'have' whose wealth knew no bounds or you were a 'have-not', who was just looking to survive. Her business exploited both segments of society. The 'haves' were her well-heeled clients and the 'have-nots' were her workers, local folks who only needed to put food on the table. If anything could be described as a perfect win-win scenario, the 'Gentlemen's After-Hours Society' would be it. Fine opium from China, bootlegged liquor and female companionship were on the menu.

But the long days at work seemed to be taking a toll on her health. A few years ago, she experienced severe back pain and a strange sensation in her leg while stooping to lift a keg full of booze. Lately, she had increasing bone pain in all of her limbs. Even the simple act of walking became a painful task. Before she was able to finish counting the day's windfall, excruciating pain developed in her thighs. When her husband lifted her from the fireplace to take her to bed, her thighs completely collapsed. Multiple fractures and deformities occurred in her ribs, spine and clavicles.

Lady Whipdale was quickly admitted to St. Thomas' Hospital across the Thames River in Southwark. Her attending physician was a Dr. Samuel Solly, who prescribed a simple bitter infusion for her failing appetite. But she got extremely frustrated with Dr. Solly and requested a more competent doctor to heal her symptoms. An additional therapy consisting of wine and arrow-root, a mutton chop and a pint of porter beer daily was recommended. When this failed, an additional infusion of orange peels, rhubarb and opium was administered. Unfortunately, this 'state-of-the-art' medicine did not succeed and she passed away a few days after admission to the hospital.

Dr. Solly conducted the autopsy which revealed multiple fractures in the ribs, legs, spine and arms. There were sections of bones that contained a 'bright red tissue matter.' Under a microscope, the red cell matter had an abnormal shape and a weird nucleus compared with healthy cells. Dr. Solly postulated that this reflected a previously undiscovered inflammatory disease process involving the 'morbid action of the blood-vessels' in which the 'earthy matter of the bone is absorbed and thrown out by the kidneys in the urine.' The first known case of multiple myeloma had been documented.

## 1847 : Calling Dr. Jones

In the year 1847, in the field of medicine, James Young Simpson discovers the anesthetic properties of chloroform and first uses it, successfully, on a patient, in an obstetric case in Edinburgh. Émile Küss and Charles-Emmanuel Sédillot performed the first recorded biopsies on neoplasms, which are abnormal and excessive growth of cellular tissues. The American Medical Association is founded in Philadelphia.

Running events were virtually non-existent, but 'pedestrian competitions', the pre-cursor to modern-day race-walking, were quite popular. It would be nearly fifty years before the first official Olympic marathon in 1896 would be won by the Greek competitor Spyridon Louis in a time of 2:58:50. The Boston Marathon was first run in April 1897, having been inspired by the revival of the marathon for the 1896 Summer Olympics in Athens, Greece. The inaugural Boston winner was John J. "JJ" McDermott, who ran the 24.5-mile course in 2:55:10, leading a field of 15 runners.

# A Black Swan Appears

Meanwhile, in England, Doctor Henry Bence Jones, a noted English physician and chemist had inadvertently dozed off in his clinic at St. George's Hospital in London. His slumber was abruptly interrupted by a knock at the door. It was his good friend Charles Darwin dropping by for a visit and a medical appointment.

"Charles, I just had the most unusual vivid dream about a black swan. All of the swans I have seen in my strolls through the park have all been of the white variety. I think that this may be an omen. The swan was trying to tell me something. I am only a humble physician. You are a renowned naturalist. What do you make of this?"

"Henry, my friend, although I cannot comment on the meaning behind your dream. A black swan sighting, be it unexpected, is not beyond the limits of understanding. Black swans were first sighted more than two hundred years ago in Australia. The swans developed a black plumage because this feature conferred a survival benefit in their specific environment. Although I don't know the exact mechanism behind this trait, this fits quite nicely with my theory of natural selection which will be published in due course."

"That is quite astonishing, and I appreciate your indulgence on this matter. Now what can I do for you? You appear to be a bit under the weather." Bence Jones realized that this was a bit of an understatement. Darwin was quite obviously suffering from ill-health and his condition seemed to be deteriorating.

Darwin quickly replied, "Since returning from the voyage on the HMS Beagle almost ten years ago, marrying my dear cousin Emma, and being mired in writing my journals, I experienced uncomfortable heart palpitations. I also recently accepted the heavy responsibility of Secretary of the Geological Society. The work stress caused me further distress, including stomach pains, boils and trembling. I fear that I may have been bitten by the kissing bug during my South America expedition." Bence Jones prescribed Darwin a daily ration of stout beer, quinine, a starvation diet and bed rest.

# The Strange Case of William Trompeur

Across town in the Marylebone district, William Trompeur, a wealthy London banker, was closing up shop after another successful business day. He had inherited his wealth and perception of the world from his father. Trompeur was dogmatic in his beliefs and rigidly stuck with the value system his father had driven into him with almost religious ferocity. As a youngster, he would be subject to much harsh discipline and verbal tongue-lashings if he did not study hard, play hard and work hard. People were not born silver spoon in hand. They were endowed with 'worthiness of character.'

Once William Trompeur began his career in the business world, there were no rules other than his very own value system to abide by. He expected to maximize profit at every opportunity, using whatever means, ethical or otherwise to increase his wealth. He would undercut his competitors, short-change his customers and pay his employees starvation wages. His understanding of the world was very simple. It is a 'just world' that we live in and people 'get what they deserved.'

And Mr. Trompeur justly deserved a vacation. Whilst on vacation, he experienced intense agonizing chest pain after taking a stumble. The local doctor was able to stabilize his condition after applying plaster to the chest area, using leach therapy to withdraw a pound of blood, and then prescribing steel and quinine.

When Trompeur returned to London, he sought treatment for his continuing symptoms of bone pain and fatigue from two renowned doctors. Drs. Macintyre and Watson gave him rhubarb and orange-peel infusions which were not effective at controlling the disease. His disease progressively worsened and as he lay dying, he took the opportunity to re-evaluate his life experience. "I was wrong about this being a just world. I certainly did not deserve this fate. Nobody deserves it." The date of Trompeur's exit from the just world was January 1, 1846.

The autopsy findings indicated that the bone marrow as 'blood-red and gelatinous' with plasma cell features. The ribs were soft, brittle and easily crumbled under the scalpel. The urine was opaque, acidic, and of a high density. A protein precipitate formed when warming the urine but redissolved when heated to 75°C; it formed again upon cooling.

Back at the residence of Dr. Henry Bence Jones, shortly after Darwin made good his leave from the premises, there was another knock at the clinic door. It was a delivery boy who handed Bence Jones a package with a note from his colleagues Drs. Macintyre and Watson. Inside the carefully wrapped package was a tube of urine. The contents of the note read as follows:

"Dear Dr. Bence Jones. As a respected chemical pathologist, you know well that we value your insights. The urine sample is from a recently deceased patient, a Mr. William Trompeur.

The enclosed tube contains a sample of said urine which is of very high specific gravity. When boiled it becomes highly opaque. On the addition of nitric acid, it effervesces, assumes a reddish hue, and becomes quite clear; but as it cools assumes the consistence of appearance which you see. Heat re-liquifies it! What is it?"

Bence Jones was intrigued with the urine sample and the prospect of unravelling the mystery. Chemistry was certainly his field of expertise and he did not want to disappoint his colleagues. He added nitric acid to the sample, re-heated the urine and then let it cool. This confirmed the results as seen by Drs. Macintyre and Watson. As for determining the exact nature of the substance, he was a bit perplexed. He ended up taking a theoretical guess and concluded that the substance was a very weird type of protein. After communicating his findings, he immediately published a scientific paper on the case study entitled 'On the new substance occurring in the urine of a patient with softening of the bone.'

His reputation for expert chemical analysis firmly intact, Dr. Bence Jones settled in for a good night's rest and dreamed again of the black swan. This time, the black swan had multiplied like a cancer into thousands of swans, each being an identical clone. The vision continued to haunt him long after he awoke. The symbolism in his dream eluded him. As a scientist, he eventually dismissed it and concluded that this dream and dreams in general were simply 'fabrications of the subconscious mind as a result of unstable chemical reactions.' According to Bence Jones, mystical explanations from the proponents of philosophy and psychology had no place in the scientific world of empirical research.

# 1873 : The Shape of Things to Come

Dr. Bence Jones certainly took the position of 'physician heal thyself' seriously. He used a stethoscope to examine his own heart palpitations. Chronic rheumatism had permanently damaged one of the valves. In early 1873, due to failing health, Bence Jones gave up his medical practice and resigned from his position as secretary to the Royal Institution of Britain.

His wife, and second cousin, Lady Millicent, was constantly by his side as Bence Jones drifted in and out of consciousness on his deathbed. He awoke briefly, uttering "My dear wife, I am not long for this world, so please indulge me for a moment. I have been to the future side and it is wonderous! The black swans now number two thousand and fifty-six. I have witnessed a beautiful spiral staircase embedded with twenty-three sparkling gemstones. The chemical composition is both intricate and elegant. But the staircase is fragile and can be undone. The damaged rungs of the ladder can be fixed. This treasure chest has but one key that unlocks all of the secrets. The meaning is clear to me now. But there is so much more to discover. The path ahead is filled with obstacles which will be overcome by science and the indomitable human spirit. My only regret is the dogmatism that clouded my thinking, ultimately blinding me to the truth."

With these final words, Bence Jones passed away peacefully, in his home at 84 Brook Street, London on April 20, 1873 at the age of 59 years. The inscription on his tombstone was simple, yet prophetic: 'The ladder of life is never-ending.' Years later, his legacy would be established as the first doctor to document the light chain protein produced by myeloma. Who knew that a little bit of urine could make one famous?

Coincidentally, the term multiple myeloma was introduced by von Rustizky the very same year that Bence Jones departed. The word myeloma is from the Greek 'myelo' - meaning 'marrow' and 'oma' meaning 'tumor.' Over the next one hundred years, progress in understanding this disease and developing therapies would proceed at a glacial pace. Similarly, the marathon is not a sprint but a carefully paced run to the finish line.

# 1885: Dr. Otto Kahler's Discovery

Life in Austria in the late 19th century was a dream-come-true for family physician Dr. Forrest Lu. He had received his medical training in Beijing, China but was forced to immigrate to Austria to escape the oppressive anti-scientific and toxic political regime of the Qing Dynasty. His flourishing medical practice in China was threatened with the attempts by the government to eliminate the opium trade.

Opium was a mainstay of therapy that he had prescribed to his patients. With this valuable resource now under attack, his livelihood was in dire jeopardy. He made enormous profits from his side-business, dealing opium 'gold' to the millions of addicts who became hooked on the drug. God bless the French and British invasions that perpetuated the opium trade in the name of free enterprise.

Regardless, the on-going persecution by the Chinese rulers eventually forced Dr. Lu to flee to Austria where he found sanctuary. He obtained his Austrian medical certification and established a family practice. His lucrative opium side-business flourished since he was able to maintain his supply pipeline from China. He viewed this as a new silk road leading directly to his doorstep. The silk road was certainly paved with gold!

In 1879, Dr. Lu, now 46 years of age, started to have severe chest pains while breathing. Fortunately, he was not only an opium dealer but a client himself. After increasing his opium intake by a ten-fold dose, he managed to control this mysterious pain that seemingly came out of nowhere.

Over the next few years, the pain had spread to his hips and spine. He became severely weak and was fatigued easily by the slightest exertion. He battled several episodes of pneumonia and suffered from anemia. His urine tests showed extremely elevated levels of an unknown protein. Finally, in 1885, through his medical contacts, he was referred to Dr. Otto Kahler, a well-respected professor of medicine and pathologist in Vienna.

By this time, Dr. Lu had experienced extreme softening of his bones and developed several fractures in his spine. He lost a significant amount of height and became quite dwarf-like in stature. Dr. Kahler was shocked to witness his colleague so grossly deformed. Having no prior knowledge of this strange disease, there was no treatment available. In 1887, Dr. Lu passed away, surviving more than 8 years, having only his best friend opium as a self-administered therapy.

Upon completion of the autopsy, Dr. Kahler's report noted the extreme deformity, softening of the bones and masses of tissue containing plasma cells. He then published the results entitled 'Symptomatology of multiple myeloma' in a Prague medical journal. Unfortunately, Dr. Kahler succumbed to tongue cancer a few years later in 1893. The mysterious illness documented in the Dr. Lu case study became known as Kahler's disease.

# 1947 : Going Insane for Urethane

There were 51 starters and a total of 41 finishers in the 1947 Boston Marathon. Yun Bok Suh of Korea was the overall winner with a then world-record performance of 2:25:39. Crossing the finish line in last place with a time of 3:02:48 was Dr. Ovido Kalboro. He was extremely proud of his achievement as he collected the coveted Boston Marathon finisher's medal in front of the Prudential Building in downtown Boston. Completing the 42.2-km course represented his ultimate quest to attain his personal holy grail, like a novice climber summiting Mount Everest. He had found his niche as a runner. It did not matter to him at all that forty more talented runners finished the race ahead of him. To Dr. Kalboro, finding one's niche in life, a place where one could claim glory and recognition, was the be-all and end-all. All else was irrelevant. The end always justified the means.

Unlike his success as a runner, his career as a medical doctor was not so stellar. Upon the conclusion of his studies and hospital internship, he had finished dead last in his class, a dubious distinction. His reputation as an incompetent cardiologist preceded him. His patients routinely succumbed to faulty procedures. Medical malpractice lawsuits became a dominate feature in his cardiology practice. His insurance premiums continued to skyrocket out of control. Dr. Kalboro desperately needed to find an exit door to escape the financial and legal madness surrounding him. He constantly pondered that there had to be a niche in the medical profession more suited to his abilities or lack thereof.

One day he stumbled upon a possible change in direction for his career path. Various medical journals were reporting case studies of blood cancers where the incidence in the general population was trending upwards. There were no viable therapies available, let alone curative strategies. One specific malady caught his attention – multiple myeloma. It was a cancer of the immune system's plasma cells which caused major bone damage, infections, hypercalcemia, kidney dysfunction and anemia.

There were few treatment options. Most folks succumbed to the disease within six months. Could this be the niche that he was searching for? If he could build a better mousetrap resulting in a viable treatment option for the disease, then fame, success and wealth would surely follow. He would become a legend in his own time! When opportunity knocks, open the door with welcoming arms!

Dr. Kalboro needed a heavy dose of inspiration, something that an intense training run would usually produce. The rush of endorphins and oxygen always gave him a mental energy boost. Solutions to once seemingly insolvable problems would appear like magic. He headed out the front door, did an easy two-kilometre warm-up jog to the local high school track and took a brief rest break before launching into his planned one-mile cruise intervals. These consisted of cruising one mile at a six-minute pace, resting for three-minutes and then repeating the sequence multiple times until exhaustion. Once he worked himself up to a total of thirteen repetitions without killing himself, he knew he would be marathon ready.

After completing his tenth repeat, a flash of inspiration flooded his brain. He suddenly remembered an old colleague, Dr. Nils Bisen-Bisquer, from his alma mater who had achieved a distinguished doctorate in chemistry, evolving into a phenomenally successful theoretical researcher in the scientific community. What if Dr. Kalboro could convince his friend to form a partnership in a business enterprise to bring a successful multiple myeloma therapy to the market? There was certainly a pent-up demand for a drug, preferably a compound that already existed and would not have to be created from scratch.

Dr. Kalboro had the business acumen and Dr. Bisen-Bisquer would provide the intellectual juice. A credible researcher who could 'manipulate data and make the science come to life' would be just what the doctor ordered. If people could be convinced of the safety and efficacy of the new drug, there would be a smooth path to profits and possibly a Nobel laureate.

After much cajoling, Dr. Bisen-Bisquer agreed to the deal. After some deliberation, it was proposed to use urethane (ethyl carbamate) to treat multiple myeloma. The advantage was that the chemical forms naturally in low quantities in many fermented foods and drinks. They concluded that intravenous infusions at low concentrations should be safe, after testing the formulation using mice. The chemical could be manufactured quite cheaply by heating urea and ethyl alcohol. The low raw material costs would ensure a healthy profit margin.

Dr. Kalboro initiated an intense advertising campaign, opened up his clinic and invited patients to receive 'the newest wonder drug of the twentieth century' to treat multiple myeloma. Soon, his medical practice was booming. He set up a holding company and named it 'Myeloma Medical Inc.' Licensing and contract agreements were signed with other medical professionals across the country. After only two years, the value of the company was sufficient to be listed as a corporation on the New York Stock Exchange.

The stock value rose steadily as Dr. Bisen-Bisquer published glowing research reports concerning the effectiveness of the urethane therapy. His writings were truly a work of an accomplished spin-master, manipulating the data to match the expectations of the stock market investors. It made for sensational reporting in the media. The newspaper headlines read, 'A miracle drug for blood cancer patients.'

The research reports were accepted into prestigious medical journals. There were anecdotal accounts of patients having a marked decrease in plasma cells in the bone marrow and an increase in hemoglobin after the urethane treatment. There was a report of a patient who discontinued nitrogen mustard and subsequently was given urethane for treatment. Because the patient experienced a 'dramatic remission', urethane therapy was administered to an additional one-hundred myeloma patients.

The research papers concluded that urethane treatments may 'bring about quite effective remissions' in chronic cases of multiple myeloma. They recorded 'striking clinical improvements' such as reduction of anemia and abnormal serum proteins. It was noted that only five of the patients died within a few months of starting therapy. The other subjects were listed as 'greatly improved' or 'improving.' The positive clinical outcomes pushed the value of the company to stratospheric levels.

One day, Dr. Kalboro received a frantic phone call from Dr. Bisen-Bisquer, who seemed to have a sense of urgency and panic in his voice. He had just received a draft copy of a study from an independent group of scientists who had tested the validity of the urethane treatment. Furthermore, their research design had incorporated a placebo control group, a new concept that was becoming the gold standard for acceptance into peer reviewed medical journals. Bisen-Bisquer remarked, "The research found that no difference in survival was demonstrated between the placebo control group and the patients receiving the therapy. Urethane was found to be toxic, carcinogenic, and largely ineffective for myeloma treatment. They recommended that urethane be withdrawn from pharmaceutical use. Once this study gets published, it will basically sink our company."

For Dr. Kalboro, this brought back memories from medical school. He recalled one of his professors commenting about the value of anecdotes (stories) in scientific research. His professor had said, "Stories are like rectums. Everybody has one and they all function in more or less the same way." The implication is that 'anecdotal evidence' is basically useless in determining cause and effect relationships. Soon, the investors will learn that the 'striking clinical improvements' promoted by Bisen-Bisquer were nothing more than a fraud.

Upon hearing the news, Dr. Ovido Kalboro had to act quickly. He owned a substantial number of shares in the company and could not afford to see his wealth evaporate before his eyes. He called his stock broker, explained the situation and got some timely advice. "Sell everything now and lock in your profits. Afterwards, sell the stock short. When the share price plummets after the bad news comes out, you can pocket the difference for a massive capital gain! The long investors will be left holding the bag."

As expected, the shares of the company became worthless after the publication of the peer reviewed reports refuting the safety and efficacy of urethane treatments. There was an investigation by the federal regulators to determine if there had been market manipulation. Congressional hearings were conducted to determine whether there was any criminal liability. Massive civil lawsuits against Myeloma Medical Inc. ensued.

Over the years, every third Monday in April on Patriots Day in Boston, Dr. Ovido Kalboro was able to view from his window, the runners on the Boston Marathon course race towards the finish line. This would evoke memories of his past race performances and he dreamed of the day he could rejoin the event. As he sat in the isolation of his jail cell, he then realized that he had finally found his niche in life.

# 1954 : Tarlac, Philippines

Just eight years after the Philippines gained its independence from the United States, Mina was born in the northern Province of Tarlac in the Philippines. Typical of that generation, Mina came from a large family with many siblings. Her family had a large plot of agricultural land that provided subsistence farming. Perhaps that is the reason Mina developed an interest in agriculture, later getting her college degree in that specialization. She studied diligently, becoming an expert in the area of fertilizers and chemicals involved in increasing efficiency in farming production. Whether this early exposure to agrichemicals was a risk factor for developing multiple myeloma would become a subject for a future debate.

Upon graduation, she realized that full-time employment in agriculture was not feasible. Like many Filipinos, she became an overseas foreign worker (OFW), taking on domestic duties with a Chinese family in Singapore. As fate would have it, in 1987, Mina eventually found domestic employment with a wonderful family in Toronto. Her employer would establish a successful housewares retail business where Mina worked tirelessly for more than 32 years, retiring only when she encountered her battle with multiple myeloma.

She became an expert in a wide range of household appliances. She also became extremely skilled in the area of home renovations, taking on many projects that she completed with the skill of a professional craftsperson. She would often lament for not 'being born a man' since her skills certainly would match the level of any male counterpart. As her partner, I always stood in awe at her natural ability to get feats of engineering done. My ability in home repair projects was decidedly inferior. I seemed to have been blessed with a 'reverse Midas touch' where everything that came my way ended up in a complete disaster.

# 1956 : How I Almost Never Came to Be

Apart from my entry into the world, 1956 was significant for the opening of the Winter Olympics in Cortina d'Ampezzo, Italy and the Summer Olympics in Melbourne, Australia. The Olympic marathon was won by Alain Mimoun of France in a time of 2:25. Antti Viskari of Finland won the Boston Marathon in a time of 2:14, a world record until the race organizers determined that the course was actually over 910 metres short.

Exactly 125 years to the day, after Darwin's voyage on the HMS Beagle from Plymouth, England, I arrived into this world, only 236 miles away in the small town of Eastbourne. My arrival into the world almost never happened. In 1945, during the allied invasion of Germany, my father, who was in the British forces, came close to losing his life when an enemy mortar shell exploded nearby, resulting in shrapnel wounds to his leg. A huge German soldier, who was in the process of surrendering, lifted my father over his shoulder and carried him to safety. To this day, I remain grateful to that soldier. Eleven years later, I entered the world.

Perhaps it was something inherited in my DNA memory that drove my interest in human evolution and cell biology. Most of the supplementary coursework that I took during university studies tended to be in the natural sciences, including Anthropology and Psychology. To this day, I am perplexed as to how I ended up with a career in finance and budgeting. Who knows, in the year 2056, I could be re-born with a renewed purpose in life, focused on participating in meaningful scientific discoveries that will contribute to the greater collective good.

Maybe the quantum theory of super-determinism has some merit to it. All events that happen, whether in the past, present or future, were pre-determined outcomes, including my own personal transformation into a multiple myeloma patient caregiver and advocate. And this new role that I find myself engulfed in, has given my life great clarity and purpose. After taking early retirement, I found myself suddenly free from the ho-hum dull-grey world of number-crunching and financial forecasting.

Suddenly, there is much more time to reflect on life's twists and turns, especially when one is forced into dealing with a potentially life-threatening disease affecting a loved one. The first reflection involves a new-found sense of spirituality. Previously, I never imagined religion or a belief in a higher power to be all that relevant. I had the naïve, yet mistaken belief, that religion and science were two separate entities. But now I realize that these are two distinct yet uniquely valuable belief systems that co-exist and are mutually dependent upon each other. After learning of Mina's diagnosis of multiple myeloma, hope and prayer became an invaluable resource in my survival toolkit, much more potent than the anti-anxiety pills my family doctor prescribed to keep me sane.

After my brain was cleared of the fog that resulted from being thrust into my new role, I embarked on a quest for rational scientific knowledge to gain a better understanding of the disease called multiple myeloma. One can learn much from the great minds who came before us as well as the current researchers who continue to build upon the foundations.

From the first documented cases of multiple myeloma in the 1840s, apart from quack treatments such as rhubarb, steel and urethane, therapy for this disease was non-existent for more than one-hundred years. Whether you are a patient or a caregiver, feel free to do your own research to give you enlightenment on new and emerging treatments. However, it is incumbent on you to always get professional advice from a qualified oncologist, preferably a hematologist who specializes in multiple myeloma.

# 1956: Confirming the Bence-Jones Protein

On the day myeloma was discovered, the doctors stood around

And they looked in amazement, at the disease they had found

They all agreed, and said this one is a clone

They knew right away, it was bad for the bones


1956 witnessed significant advances in science, technology and medicine. Academics from MIT, Bell Labs and IBM assemble the first coordinated research meeting on the topic of artificial intelligence. The hard disk drive is invented by an IBM team. The Asian flu pandemic originates in China. HeLa cells became the first human cell line that could grow and divide endlessly in a laboratory, leading scientists to label these cells 'immortal.' These cells have played a key role in some of the major advances in fields such as cancer biology. The year also saw the emergence of the first photographic images of the DNA molecule.

It was not until 1956 that scientists finally were able to decode that mysterious protein discovered in the urine by Dr. Henry Bence Jones well over 100 years ago. The relationship between the Bence-Jones protein found in the urine and the proteins found in the blood of multiple myeloma patients was demonstrated in a study performed by Korngold and Lipari. They discovered two main classes of Bence-Jones protein secreted by the cancerous plasma cells in the bone marrow. These proteins became known as kappa and lambda. These proteins exist in the blood of healthy individuals within a normal range. If either one is present in the urine, even in small quantities, this is a marker of the disease. Myeloma cancer cells will produce an over-abundance of either kappa or lambda, never both and sometimes neither.

I am astounded how some folks will use kappa and lambda terminology as if they were suddenly endowed with medical expertise. Monday morning myeloma quarterbacks abound in the hospital waiting rooms. I overheard a conversation between two myeloma patients who were discussing the diagnosis of a fellow patient. "Oh, he has the kappa version of the disease. His prognosis definitely does not look good!" The other patient nodded her head approvingly, seemingly to give some efficacy to the statement.

Later, I had the opportunity to discuss this statement with one of the nurse practitioners. I asked, "Does the diagnosis of either kappa or lambda myeloma confer a worse prognosis for this type of protein found in the urine?" Her response was an emphatic "No." I suppose that when people are faced with a life-threatening crisis such as cancer, they feel that their lives are out of control. They look for answers amidst the chaos and panic thrust upon them. Coming up with their own pseudo-scientific theories may help them regain a sense of control.

As our nurse practitioner explained to us, the kappa and lambda proteins are nothing more than markers of the output of the cancer cells. Other than helping us monitor the impact of the treatment and the disease progression, they have no greater significance beyond that.

This explanation seemed to make sense to me. From my psychology studies, I learned that our brains have to process multiple stimuli from the environment on a daily basis. But our brains are not super computers. We can only process tiny bits of information bombarding us. Hence, there is a need for the brain to selectively filter information and categorize it. This allows us to make sense of our world, albeit in a conveniently compartmentalized fashion. For example, classifying kappa and lambda into a simplistic 'good' versus 'evil' scenario, provides some sort of closure to the internal psychological conflicts operating within one's consciousness.

The same kind of psychological processes happened during the COVID-19 pandemic. We have all witnessed the mass panic and hoarding of toilet paper and other critical supplies when the lockdowns occurred. Other folks dealt with the pandemic by denying it and refusing to wear masks. Even empirical science-based data and advice from the experts could not convince them of the reality. Given this, it is not at all surprising that a life-threatening cancer diagnosis will drive people into a survival mode of thinking. This can result in the denial of reality or the outright invention of a new reality, one that is structured to soothe the psyche.

The initial discoveries that began with Dr. Henry Bence Jones and Dr. Otto Kahler had evolved into a deeper understanding of the disease. The significance of this research cannot be understated. Scientists would later develop specialized tests and procedures to diagnose multiple myeloma and monitor the effectiveness of treatment using these key kappa and lambda protein markers in the blood and urine.

## 1990s : One Very Tough Competitor

水滴石穿: 'Persistent effort overcomes any difficulty'

For the past twenty-six years, I have been running consistently, with about four thousand kilometres of total mileage each year, with an estimated cumulative total of one hundred and four thousand kilometres. To put this into perspective, it equates to a distance of approximately 2.6 times around the circumference of the earth.

I began running to get into basic shape after years of letting my health deteriorate and my weight balloon to the point where my body mass index indicated a level of obesity. In 1994, I joined the local YMCA, at first joining aerobic classes to get my weight under control and eventually transitioning to the indoor running track to burn even more calories. After five months, I went from 185 pounds right down to 139 pounds.

People at my workplace noticed the drastic transformation and wanted to know if I had caught some type of insidious cancer that was eating away at my body. When I returned to my dentist for routine cleaning, he looked concerned and also inquired if my health was an issue. I am sure that he assumed that I had contracted HIV and was deeply concerned for my health.

## 1995 : Becoming A Marathoner

In May 1995, I ran my first marathon, the Shoppers Drug Mart Toronto Marathon, finishing in the respectable time of three hours and six minutes. One year later, I cracked the three-hour gold standard for marathoners, running a 2:59 at the Friendly Massey Marathon. In 1998, I ran in the City of Scarborough Bi-centennial five-kilometre race, winning it outright in 18 minutes and 23 seconds. I successfully qualified for and ran in five Boston Marathons, with a personal best time of 3:01.

## Moving Up to The Ultra Marathon

A few years later, not satisfied with being a mere marathon runner, I transitioned into ultra running, defined as races from 50-km right up to 10-day running events. I won several 24-hour races, a 6-hour race, and a two-day Ultimate Canuck race. I won the Ontario Ultra Series and the Western New York State Ultra series. I competed for Team Canada in the 24-Hour World Championships in France (2010) and the Netherlands (2013). I also secured some Canadian age-group ultra running records. In just a very short period of time, I went from a total couch potato to a competitive level of running. I felt that I had 'arrived' and that the world was my running oyster.

## Recording Daily Progress

As most runners are obsessive-compulsive, I faithfully logged every single day of my training in a hand-written journal. I recorded not just my daily mileage but other key variables such as the running route, outdoor temperature, body weight, indoor track workouts, race results, nutrition, people I trained with and any dreaded injuries that sidelined my training. Precise record-keeping, I reasoned, would allow me to review past training and replicate successes and avoid future failures.

I hoped that these journals would survive me long after I departed planet Earth and become entrenched in some sort of historical reference for my ancestors to enjoy and emulate. Everyone wants a monument to themselves after death. This was my own unique way of becoming immortal. Mina even built me a massive board to affix all the medals that I earned from my races, everything from 5-km races to 24-hour ultra-marathons. She called it 'Paul's Running Wall of Fame.'

The office in our home was transformed into my own personal trophy room. She supported me at every race that I competed in, even setting up a tent next to the 24-hour race courses that I ran in, encouraging me throughout the race and waking up the next morning to continue to cheer me on. And then, eventually, the time on the race clock arrived for me to support her as a full-time caregiver.

## A Disease of Excellence

Little did I realize how valuable this running obsession would be later in life as I evolved into a multiple myeloma patient advocate and caregiver. Multiple myeloma is a disease of the plasma cells, but a running injury, as the late running guru Doctor George Sheehan describes it, is a 'Disease of Excellence.' In many respects, surviving a running race and surviving multiple myeloma have much in common.

However, this book is not about myself and my running achievements. It is a story of Mina's strength and resilience in the face of a very tough competitor – multiple myeloma. She never dropped out of the race no matter how much pain and suffering she endured. She became tougher than the strongest ultra-marathon runner that I had ever known.

## 2001 Our First Competitor : Thyroid Cancer

如釋重負: 'To feel freed of a great burden'

After my first marriage had failed, I met Mina in 2001, through an on-line dating website. Her profile name was 'Simple Lady at 46.' Without the invention of the internet, Mina and I would never have met each other. We are now celebrating twenty-years together with plans to celebrate another twenty years in retirement.

The internet was quite a new phenomenon at the time. The running community was using it extensively, mainly to register for upcoming races and to search for the latest training advice. GPS running watches, which would introduce revolutionary technology to track mileage and athletic performance were becoming popular. I resisted adopting the new technology, preferring to stick with my trusty old-fashioned Timex chrono watch, recording my daily workouts in a hand written running journal. Being a financial and budget analyst for most of my career, I was comfortable with the pen and paper approach. We financial types love to write things down.

# The 2001 Boston Marathon

In 2001, Lee Bong-ju of South Korea won the men's race in the 105<sup>th</sup> Boston Marathon

in a time of 2:09:43 and Catherine Ndereba of Kenya was the women's winner with a time of

2:23:53. That year, I took a break from running that race, having completed it in four previous

years.

The year 2001 marked seven years of running for myself. With the emotional trauma of

divorce hanging over my head, I only had the will to participate in one running event that year,

the Toronto Scotiabank Half-Marathon. The previous year, I had run my fourth Boston

Marathon, with my all-time best Boston time of 3:01. I had also 'tested the waters' of the ultra-

marathon distance, running my first ultra at the Kingston Sri Chinmoy six-hour race, with a

respectable distance of 68 kilometres, finishing in fifth place overall. I thought that I would go

crazy running one-kilometre loops around historic Fort Frederick, but it turned out to be great

fun and I subsequently became hooked.

Regular running training programs and intense race competitions do wonderous things

for both your stamina and the immune system. Not only does your cardiovascular system

become super-charged, but the entire immune system contained in the bone marrow gets a huge

boost. The bone marrow contains stem cells. The stem cells can develop into the red blood cells

that carry oxygen through your body, the white blood cells that fight infections, and the platelets

that help with blood clotting. Running, and basically any kind of high-intensity aerobic exercise,

provides preventative maintenance for one's immune system and is the simplest strategy you can

employ to guard against all kinds of diseases, including cancer.

There are no guarantees. On rare occasions, runners can also get cancer, including

multiple myeloma. But exercise and healthy diet modifications tend to tilt the odds in a very positive direction. You can load the dice in your favor. This is an important consideration to keep in mind, especially if you find yourself in the role of a patient caregiver. My family doctor once provided me with an interesting analogy. He said, "Paul, when you are flying on an airplane and the oxygen masks get deployed, the number one rule is to take care of yourself first, put on your own oxygen mask, save yourself and then you can assist others."

If you suddenly find yourself in the role of a caregiver to a loved one who is a cancer patient, it is very easy to let this affect you psychologically. The classic symptoms of denial, anger and depression can overwhelm you. If you are not physically fit, you will likely have a very tough time managing the essential care that your loved one needs and deserves. On the other hand, if you take care of your own physical health, the emotional rollercoaster becomes manageable and less daunting. Physical fitness, in short, translates into emotional well-being.

# An Old Car, Dinner and a Movie

For our first meeting, Mina sent me an email message indicating that she would pick me up at the subway station and then we would go for dinner and a movie. She gave me the license plate of her car so that I could look out for her when she arrived at the station. Apparently, she would be driving a luxury Mercedes SUV. As she finally drove into the station, to my surprise and disappointment, the car was a beat-up second-hand Ford Tempo. I thought to myself that either I had written down the wrong license plate number or Mina has a wicked sense of humor. The latter case proved to be true.

It was quite a memorable first date. Mina is from the Philippines, as coincidentally, was my ex-wife. We watched Brad Pitt and Julia Roberts in 'The Mexican', an OK action-adventure comedy, but a bit too long to sit through. Runners have legs that tend to cramp up from extended sitting and my muscles were no exception. After watching the film, we had a less than auspicious lunch together at a local restaurant.

At this point in my life, I had adopted a healthy vegetarian diet for at least the past fifteen years. The high carbohydrate diet fit perfectly into my running lifestyle. Carbs are the main fuel source that runners burn during aerobic exercise, followed by fats and proteins. Knowing my nutritional requirements, Mina ordered a special salad for my lunch. Of course, the restaurant was primarily a meat-eaters paradise and so they produced a salad that 'did not quite perform up to expectations.' In other words, they totally screwed up the vegetarian salad that I ordered.

Despite some bumps along the way, Mina and I became a team. We were both positive influences on each other, especially when it came to modification of diets and adopting a regular exercise routine. She became my main support at various running events, faithfully providing encouragement and praise as I crossed the finish line in many marathons, half-marathons, ten-kilometre and five-kilometre events. She even registered for a 5-km Canada Day race with me, with both of us winning age group medals and a lunch voucher at a local restaurant.

# 2001 : Our First Medical Crisis

Later in the fall of 2001, Mina's family doctor noticed a lump and swelling in her neck. She was sent for a series of blood work and ultrasound tests. We received the diagnosis about one week later – thyroid cancer. Upon learning of this news, naturally we were both shocked and in some distress. I quickly headed to the internet to Google as much information as my scientifically deficient brain could absorb on the subject of thyroid cancer.

People tend to thrive on information, especially when it comes to determining cause and effect relationships. This is likely tied into our evolutionary success as a species. Knowledge is power, which gives you predictability and increases your odds of survival in high-risk environments. With thyroid cancer, I gained some comfort knowing that it is one of the most curable types of cancer with an estimated 10-year survival rate of 96%. Although most thyroid tumours are benign, Mina's was malignant.

Mina had one of the most common types of thyroid cancer – papillary. According to Thyroid Cancer Canada, this type of cancer tends to grow very slowly. Although they grow slowly, papillary cancers often spread to the lymph nodes in the neck. Even when these cancers have spread to the lymph nodes, they can often be treated successfully and are rarely fatal. The thyroid gland is a critical organ. A cancerous thyroid must be treated quickly to avoid long-term harm.

Mina went through the entire battery of tests leading up to the thyroid cancer diagnosis at St. Michaels' Hospital in Toronto. There was an ultrasound test which found the solid tumours in the thyroid itself and they also checked the nearby lymph nodes to see if the cancer had spread. Mina had a biopsy to retrieve a tissue sample. She also swallowed a radioactive iodine pill. The doctor explained that the iodine would eventually get absorbed into the thyroid gland and a special camera scan would then be used. The tissue biopsy combined with the camera scan was used to confirm the cancer diagnosis.

The treatment for thyroid cancer typically involves the complete surgical removal of the thyroid gland and the neighboring lymph nodes, which the doctors recommended for Mina. We were warned in advance that this would involve at least a one week stay in the hospital and several weeks of extended recovery after that. Her family doctor also said that she would be totally wiped out and fatigued for several weeks after the surgery. Mina was forced to take leave without pay from her retail manager's position. Fortunately, she did have some additional medical insurance to help reimburse some expenses and she was able to use unused vacation to help offset the time-off from her employment.

After the surgery was completed, I headed directly to her recovery room at St. Michael's Hospital. One of her friends had made it there before me and was comforting her. The sight of seeing your loved one almost totally incapacitated in a hospital bed was distressing to say the least. This being a totally new experience for myself, I was totally unprepared and did not have a clue about playing the role of an effective caregiver, let alone a patient advocate.

The doctors had warned that Mina might lose her voice since the surgery sometimes causes collateral damage to the voice box. However, when she awoke after the procedure, the first thing she said was "I want Swiss Chalet chicken."

# A Long Road to Recovery

Three months after the surgery, she was confined in hospital for three days and quarantined due to further treatment of radioactive iodine pills. Absolutely no contact was permitted and food was slid under the hospital room door. All of her clothes that she had worn to the hospital had to be thrown away once she was released. One year later she was given a second set of iodine pills and had to isolate in the hospital again. When she did return back home, I joked that we would never need a night-light in our bedroom again since she glowed in the dark.

She managed to return to work after four weeks of recovery. For the next several years, she went for annual ultrasound scans and routine blood tests to ensure that the cancer had not spread to any of the remaining lymph nodes. She was given the all-clear at every subsequent annual appointment.

Fortunately, thyroid hormone replacement therapy is available and allows patients to live quality lives. Mina was prescribed a daily dose of levothyroxine. Mina's family doctor carefully monitored her while she was on this medication since improper dosing can result in serious side effects. It was all about achieving a proper balance.

# Balance in Running

Runners know all about 'balance.' We regularly take nutritional supplements, electrolytes (minerals that help balance water and acidity levels) and other medicines to optimize our training and running performance. Misuse of what we ingest can have serious or even fatal consequences. For example, too much water hydration during an intense marathon race can result in hyponatremia, which is a low sodium concentration in the blood. About 10% of folks participating in endurance events may experience a significant imbalance in electrolytes.

We were totally relieved to finish treatment, but we found it hard not to worry about the cancer growing or coming back. Learning to live with cancer that does not go away can be difficult and very stressful, a reality that multiple myeloma patients know all too well. Mina did very well after treatment, but her endocrinologist said that due to the radioactive iodine treatment there was a small risk of developing a secondary cancer. There are conflicting research studies concerning this risk. There is some evidence to suggest an increased risk of blood and salivary gland cancers which may be linked to radioactive iodine therapy.

My experience as a runner helped us through our thyroid cancer experience. Runners learn how to deal with setbacks and failures, just as Mina coped with her cancer diagnosis. Runners get injured and sometimes have to drop out of a race competition. But we never give up. Cancer patients have a similar level of perseverance, determination and resilience. We modify our training and treatment plan and listen to the medical experts. We learn from our experiences and then look forward to greater achievements in the future. We have faith and hope that a cancer cure is just around the corner.

We both gave our thanks to God for helping us through this first competition. It was a huge relief to cross the finish line and collect our finishers medals. It felt like a thousand-pound weight was lifted from our shoulders and we were freed of a great burden. Little did we know that this was not the end, it was just the beginning. This was just a minor 100-yard sprint compared to the ultra-marathon that we would face years later.

## 2018 Our Second Competitor : Mucoepidermoid Cancer

雷打不動：  'To be determined, unshakable'

The 2018 Winter Olympics are held in Pyeongchang, South Korea. The Boston Marathon was held as usual, on Patriots Day in April. Yuki Kawauchi of Japan won the 122nd Boston Marathon men's race in 2:15:58 and Desiree Linden of the United States won the women's race in 2:39:54.

Cancer research took some gigantic leaps during 2018. There were several scientific articles which outlined that simple lifestyle changes, such as diet and exercise, that could dramatically reduce cancer risk. There were new insights into the relationship between obesity and cancer, which indicated that fatty accumulation in the immune cells compromised the body's ability to defend itself against cancer. Amazingly, researchers created nanorobots that can be programmed to shrink tumors by obstructing their blood supply.

## 2003 : Running the Boston Marathon

It had been three years since my last Boston Marathon appearance. Mina and my daughter Sophia had accompanied me to the 2003 race. We took a side trip to Rhode Island to do the Newport Mansions tour. The night before the race, we celebrated with dinner at an Italian restaurant in Boston's Back Bay area. Early the next morning, Mina and Sophia saw me off at the Boston Commons where I boarded the shuttle bus which took me to the start line, 26.2 miles away in Hopkinton.

I ran a decent race in 2003, giving it my all, running with determination and unshakable confidence, finishing in 3:10:48. There was nothing sweeter than finishing my 5th Boston Marathon. I felt like I was the luckiest guy on earth, collecting the race medal and being cheered on by Mina and Sophia. Having a support crew at a big race event is just like having your own personal caregivers at your side, to help you through the pain and celebrate the victories. Success in running is similar to a remission in multiple myeloma. You may get many years of consistent running before you 'relapse.' You then have to deal with an injury, extended downtime and depression when you realize that you are not invincible.

# The Pain of Ultra Marathon Running

I had ambitious running plans for 2018, signing up for the entire Ontario Ultra Marathon series. The races ranged from 50-km events to a 24-hour endurance run around a 1-km course. The organizers give you points for every successful race completed and bonus points depending on how close to first place you get. I had won the entire series in my younger years, but would settle for a finish in the top three this year.

The first event was the 50-km Pick Your Poison trail race at the end of April. The week before the race, I developed a very bad case of bronchitis. The walk-in clinic doctor told me not to run. I scratched that race and I ended up with a DNS (Did Not Start). What a disappointing way to begin the season! Anyway, the event turned out to be a disaster, with all of the snow and ice accumulation, very few runners finished. The Seaton Soaker 50-km trail race was next on the agenda. I managed to finish that in 6:37 with some difficulty since the bronchitis cough slowed me down. I then headed to Massachusetts in late May to do the Watuppa 50-km trail race, finishing in 5:27. One week later, I completed the Sulphur Springs 50-miler in 11:16.

Mina was working on my race day Saturdays and could not accompany me. But I always had her in my mind as I was struggling up some very tough trail hills. I imagined her cheering me on like she usually did at previous events that we went to. As soon as I returned home from the competitions, she would enthusiastically greet me and then proudly displayed my finishing on my running wall of fame.

In the first week of June, I competed in the 6-Hour Sri Chinmoy race in Kingston, Ontario. Again, Mina was at work and so I travelled solo to the event. The course was a one-kilometre loop around the grounds of historic Fort Frederick, one of my favourite races and brought back fond memories of being my very first ultra marathon competition more than ten years ago. I finished in eleventh place with 54.9 kilometres, not my best effort but better than expected, given that my bronchitis cough had returned with a vengeance.

The second week of June saw the start of a two-day Ultimate Canuck event. Competitors have to run 50-km on Saturday and then complete a 42.2-km marathon on the next day. I finished the 50-km in 5:15 and the marathon in 4:27, winning first place overall in the Men's age 60 to 69 division. Along with the race medals, I brought home two bottles of wine. By this point, I was already in the top three in the Ontario series. Things were starting to look brighter, both with my training and my race performances.

The week following was the Niagara 100-km Ultra. I ran the first 50-km, pacing myself at a six minute per kilometre clip with my ultra running teammate Charlotte. For the final half of the race, I did my best to keep up with her, but started to wilt under the heat of the midday sun. I managed to finish in a respectable 11:17 and ninth place overall, only slowing down modestly and winning my age group.

## Maintaining Balance

For the next events at the end of June and in July, Mina finally had the weekend off from work and was able to travel with me. First on the agenda was the Pure Grit 52.5-km in Tobermory. It was a long drive and we got to Wiarton late at night, making it to the town's only Chinese restaurant just before closing time. The next day, I had a less than stellar running performance, finishing seven loops of the 7.5-km trail course in ninth place with a time of 6:53. I suppose all of the heavy duty mileage I had accumulated through training and previous races was starting to catch up to me.

Intense cancer therapy is similar to an intense running program. Whether it is high dose chemo drugs, radiation or surgery, the side-effects of the treatment program sometimes catches-up with the patient. If a balance is not maintained between 'not enough' and 'too much', the therapy is sometimes worse than the disease itself.

# Mina - My Personal Race Support and Caregiver

In the first week of July, it was the Limberlost Challenge 56-km trail race, a very scenic but tough trail course. I finished the four loops of 14-km in 8:27, good enough for first place in my seniors age group division. Mina sat patiently at the start/finish, cheering me on and taking photos as I went past her each loop. Her excitement and enthusiasm were contagious.

We both looked forward to another of my favourite races at the end of July, the 24-Hour Sri Chinmoy race in Ottawa, the oldest continuously running 24-Hour race in the world. It is run on a 1.8-kilometre loop around a college. I had won this event in three previous years in 2008, 2010, and 2017. As she did in previous versions of this event, Mina set up a tent and table trackside. She took care of me right from the 9 a.m. race start up to 11 p.m. when she had to retire for the night to get some sleep. My race did not go as I expected, as there are a ton of things that can go wrong at a 24-Hour race. I finished seven hours early at two in the morning, with a total of 131.551 kilometres and 13th place overall. We drove the four-hour trip back to Toronto, excitedly talking about our plans to celebrate our upcoming three year wedding anniversary in September, which was also Mina's birthday.

In mid-August, I entered two events in Massachusetts. I ran a very tough 50-km race at the East End Trail Races at the Borderland State Park, finishing in a slow 7:35.  Next was the Sweltering Summer Ultra Marathon, which is an eight-hour event around a track in Clapp Park (yes, it sounds like a strange name for a park) in Pittsfield, Massachusetts. I followed behind my Canadian teammate Charlotte, hoping to get some free pacing since I knew her goal was to get a personal best with about 80-km for the 8-hour race. We were running consistent 3:10 laps. I felt quite comfortable at this pace. They had a huge pair of speakers in the middle of the field blasting out music which was really motivational.

The Canadians in this race took away most of the awards. Charlotte ended up being the top female. I finished in eight-place with almost 46 miles, winning the Men's 60 to 69 age division and getting a very nice customized wooden plaque. At the end of August, I completed the Green Lakes Endurance 50-km race near Syracuse, New York in 5:27.

# The Emergence of a Second Cancer Crisis

During that summer, Mina's dentist noticed a bump on the floor of her mouth when Mina went for a routine dental check-up. The dentist arranged for her to have a free biopsy done at a local college dental school. We booked the appointment but were very disappointed with the outcome. The student dentists obviously did not have a clue as to what they were doing. The attempt at a routine biopsy was a dismal failure. Oh well, what can one expect from a 'free' service?

We immediately contacted Mina's family doctor who provided a referral to the Mount Sinai Hospital Head and Neck clinic. We were seen by Doctor Eric Monteiro, a top specialist in his field. He took some diagnostic imaging scans and expertly extracted a tissue sample from the floor of Mina's mouth. The CT scan also indicated some possible lesions on the pancreas that would require a follow-up scan in six months.

We returned for a follow-up appointment the next week to get the results. We were hoping and praying for a benign diagnosis but secretly feared the worst case scenario. The doctor instantly gave us the bad news. It was a cancerous tumour in the soft tissue on the bottom left side of the mouth, called mucoepidermoid carcinoma or cancer of the salivary gland. He said, "The good news is that this is a really low-grade type of cancer which has a very good prognosis. The bad news is that it is located in a difficult spot. The surgery to remove the tumour will cut the nerves to your tongue which will result in a permanent speech impediment. You will have difficulty with your pronunciation and this will probably result slurred speech."

We were both devastated by this news and tried to make sense of it. Dr. Monteiro indicated that it is the most common malignancy observed in the major and minor salivary glands. Prior exposure to ionizing radiation appears to substantially increase the risk of developing malignant cancer of the major salivary glands, particularly mucoepidermoid carcinoma.

Our oncologists gave us some reason for optimism. Generally, there is a good prognosis for low-grade tumours, and a poor prognosis for high-grade ones. Surgery is the recommended treatment for localised disease. After surgery, if there are positive margins with cancer cells still present, the radiation oncologist told us that post-operative radiotherapy can effectively remove any residual cancer cells.

# Vacation Getaway and More Races

Mina's surgery for the salivary gland cancer was promptly scheduled for the end of September, 2018. Despite this, we decided to go ahead with our annual combined wedding anniversary and Mina's birthday vacation getaway. Each year, we try to go to a different destination, some place where we have never been before. On this occasion, we chose to visit Pelee Island and Point Pelee National Park, the lowest point in Canada.

The trip to Pelee Island, in the middle of Lake Erie, took about ninety minutes on the ferry. We had a wonderful time, exploring the local museum and history. I had a bit too much wine during the wine tasting at the Pelee Island Winery. Mina had to drive the car when we toured around the island afterwards. We had a great dinner at one of the local restaurants before heading back to the mainland on the ferry. The next day, we completed a tour of Point Pelee National Park. With cancer surgery on the horizon, this was the last vacation we would have together for the foreseeable future.

I had two more race events to complete in September before Mina's scheduled surgery. The first was the Haliburton Forest 50-mile trail race, a tough course and definitely not for the inexperienced runner. Of course, given Mina's condition she did not come with me to the race. I tried my best to focus on running my best, but I simply could not. My head was simply not going to let me. I ended up tripping up multiple times on tree roots and rocks, basically doing 'face-plants.' Finally, halfway into the event, I decided to run with one of the more experienced trail runners, which helped pass the time.

I finished in 11 hours and 32 minutes and 32nd place overall, more than two hours slower than when I previously run this race. I was just grateful to cross the finish line and collect my medal. You can see how one's emotional state can impact running performance. The psychological impact of Mina's cancer diagnosis was also beginning to affect my performance at work. Budgeting and financial planning are difficult tasks even with a clear mind. The stress from suddenly being placed in a position of patient caregiver started to wear me down at work.

# The North Coast Race : 24 Hours in Cleveland

Two weeks later, I headed to Cleveland, Ohio to compete in the North Coast 24-Hour USA Championships. I car-pooled with my friend Charlotte, who is one of the top women in the Canadian ultra running community. Her friend Monica, another elite level ultra-marathon athlete, went with us to provide track-side support. As I expressed doubts after my poor performances in recent races, Charlotte boosted my spirits with some words of inspiration. She said, "Don't worry Paul, I know your ability. I have seen you in action at the eight-hour ultra in Pittsfield and you will do awesome in this race!"

The past week had been quite a blur and so I wasn't sure if I could get my head straight to run 24 hours with all of the recent stress and turmoil surrounding Mina's cancer diagnosis. And then it became clear to me how the therapeutic value of running 24 hours helps 'clear the fog' from life's daily challenges and helps to strengthens one's psychological and physical focus ten-fold more than any anti-anxiety drug could possibly do. Running is the ultimate coping mechanism that provides you with the toolkit to save yourself in order to help others.

Running an ultra-marathon is analogous in many ways to the challenges that we all face in life. There is the multi-month training regimen that leads up to the big event, maintenance of a healthy weight and diet and injury avoidance. Sometimes we all do just the right things, proper nutrition, exercise, stress reduction, avoidance of alcohol and tobacco, taking your blood pressure meds religiously and attending regular family doctor appointments. But sometimes, life throws you a curveball or a speedbump, despite the fact that you followed all of the rules, disciplined yourself to the maximum and lead a life of absolute purity. Perhaps you may have run 10 kilometers too many during a training run that resulted in an injury or in Mina's case had the misfortune of dealing with uncontrollable factors such as genetics.

But the strong continue, they persist, and they adapt despite these setbacks. In doing so, you gain strength from your inner self as well as from all of the social network of family and friends that are there to support you. This might sound cliched, but the destination, not the finish line is the most important goal. The journey along the way is a long one. It sometimes forces you to take a different path, but you eventually get there, with the help of your own inner attitude, an army of friends to cheer you on and a good GPS to help you pace on the road.

Needless to say, during the 5-hour drive to Cleveland, my mind tried to focus on the upcoming race but I just could not get my head in gear. But travelling with Charlotte and Monica, two very accomplished women ultra-runners settled me down. About 60% of the discussion centered around running but the other 40% was about work, personal life and the challenges we all face outside of running.

On race day, we all lined up at the start, they played the American anthem and we were off and running. At about seven hours, my legs felt that they were totally trashed and I started to walk. After 90 minutes of walk-recovery, Monica gave me two extra strength Advil and I started to run again. After the first lap, I passed by Monica and said "I can feel the Advil starting to kick in." It was amazing. The ibuprofen totally eliminated the inflammation in my running muscles and I started to run at a very fast clip, more than the 10-km per hour than when I started the race. As I lapped Charlotte, who was now at least 6 laps ahead of me, she yelled "Go Paul, wow, you are just an animal." I was now a man with a mission and I could feel the adrenaline surge. The emotion that I felt was directly related to life's unfairness at the deck of cards that Mina had be dealt. Perhaps I was still in the anger-denial stage, but this race had given me an outlet, with a gigantic cathartic release of energy.

The sun started to rise over Lake Erie and the countdown to the end of the race began. There was an electronic lap counter at the start/finish line that records your laps and mileage as you cross the timing mat. I saw Charlotte cross ahead of me and noticed that I had erased the multi-lap deficit she gained on me during the race. With about 40 minutes remaining, Charlotte ran up beside me and told me to "go for it if I wanted to kick her ass in the race." I thought to myself that I wasn't really here to compete against Charlotte, just to attain my own personal goals of stress relief and healing. But at the end of the day, I thought, "OK, why not since, after all, it is a race." For the remaining time, I turned on my after-burners and ran as hard as I could. The horn sounded to end the race. I finished in 7th place overall with 118.8 miles or more than 191 kilometres. Charlotte finished right behind me in 8th place overall with 118.6 miles. After the race, it was a very long drive back to Toronto.

Another 24-hour race was now history and in the books. As I have commented before, running mimics life in many ways. This race was especially relevant in that respect. I learn something new as a runner in every event, no matter that I have been running for 26 years. Often life presents roadblocks that can either defeat you or you can jump over or run around. This race was no exception. At one point, I almost gave up but then my mind focused on Mina, who was not giving up. And that gave me all the power I needed to continue.

# Oral Cancer Surgery

September of 2018 marked the start of our oral cancer journey. I had taken stress leave from work and would not be returning until further notice. My family doctor had given me authorization for the leave and a prescription for Ativan, for stress relief and Zopiclone, to help me sleep. He said that I would not be much use at the office with my emotional state in a complete state of flux.

Previously, the routine I had for work, getting up at 5 a.m., prioritizing my work, setting up meetings and so forth, all now became background noise and quickly faded from my memory. It's funny how some things that were previously of critical importance now seemed to be largely irrelevant.

On September 24, 2018, we had to prepare for the upcoming cancer surgery to remove the salivary gland tumour. The check-in at Mount Sinai Hospital was non-eventful. The doctors and nursing staff briefed us on the planned procedures. First, Doctor Monteiro would use his expertise to surgically remove the tumour. After the removal of the cancer, a second specialist, Doctor De Almeida, would replace the tissue removed from the floor of the mouth with a skin transplanted from Mina's arm. The arm tissue would be replaced by a transplant of tissue from Mina's thigh. After they assisted Mina to the operating room, the hospital staff advised me to go home and wait for telephone updates from the doctors. I departed the hospital knowing that this was the last time I would hear Mina speak normally.

Early in the afternoon, Doctor Monteiro called me and indicated the cancer surgery was successful and that he was able to remove the tumour completely. This was reassuring since it meant that post-surgery radiotherapy would probably not be necessary. He told me to expect another call from Doctor De Almeida later in the day, to give me an update on the tissue transplant procedure which would provide a flap for the area in Mina's mouth where the cancer was removed. A few hours later, the doctor called and indicated that the procedure was successfully completed. I could now head back to the hospital to visit Mina in the intensive care unit.

Later in the day, I arrived at the Mount Sinai Hospital intensive care unit. It was certainly distressing to see Mina in her post-operative state. She was conscious but had a hole in her throat with an attached feeding tube, which had to be suctioned at regular intervals. I stayed in the unit with her for as long as possible, returning home to get some sleep, waking early the next morning to get back down to the hospital.

Her recovery in the ICU was difficult. Most of the nursing staff responded well and assisted her with nutrition and suctioning the feeding tube. There was only one night where she got into distress and could not convince the on-duty nurse to provide suction to the tube. The nurse indicated that the machine showed sufficient oxygen intake and so there was no need for suctioning. As Mina's significant other and primary caregiver, I was naturally upset with this news and I vowed to stay with her full-time in the hospital to ensure that I would be there to advocate for her needs.

# My First Test as a Caregiver

After three days in the intensive care unit, she was moved to her own recovery room in the hospital. Although my medical insurance plan covered only semi-private hospital stays, to minimize the risk of possible infection, Mina had to be assigned a private room. I brought a small bag with a change of clothes and my tablet computer. I stayed with her in the hospital 24/7. There was just enough room in the bed for me to lie beside her.

The doctors and nurses from the Head and Neck unit woke us early each morning and checked Mina's surgery wounds and vitals. The surgery wounds on her left arm and thigh looked terrible, totally blackened with scabs. But the doctors indicated that this was normal and the healing process was proceeding well. After a few days, the feeding tube was removed and a small patch was placed over the wound in her throat. She had to keep tapping on the patch to encourage the throat wound to heal.

During our recovery stay in the hospital, Melanie and Alan, some of our friends from the running group, the Fast Friends as we are aptly named, dropped by to visit and offer encouragement. The importance of having good friends that form part of one's support group cannot be underestimated. My daughter Sophia and her husband Carlo also visited. They were an important family component of the social support group equation. I viewed their role as caregivers as critical, with equal importance as my own duty as a patient caregiver and advocate.

After about ten days, we were transferred to a ward unit in the hospital with three other patients. By this point, Mina was well on her way to recovery. The wound in her throat was healing but there was a noticeable indentation where the feeding tube had entered into the esophagus. Doctor Monteiro said he could repair it in an outpatient clinic in about six months. He wanted to give Mina more healing time and reduce the risk of infection from additional surgery. Mina also developed a post-surgery shingles infection which required treatment with two daily doses of acyclovir, an anti-viral medication.

Thankfully, we only had to spend one night in the ward unit. The next day, the doctors gave us the all clear and Mina was discharged from the hospital at noon. The real challenge now was placed on myself as a full-time caregiver, along with Mina's friend Mila, who lives with us. Since Mina's swallowing function was still severely compromised, we had to make special meals, which were basically liquid in nature. I made regular trips to the pharmacy to buy a special protein powder to mix in with Mina's liquid meals.

# Struggle to the Finish Line

It was now the first week of October and I still had three race events remaining in the Ontario Ultra series. Mina encouraged me to finish the series since I had already registered and I was still in contention to finish in the top three. The Sticks and Stones 50-km trail race was held at the Christie Lake Conservation Area in Dundas, Ontario. The course is a 5-km loop around a small lake, which competitors must repeat ten times to successfully complete the race. My leg muscles were still sore from the intense effort of the 24-Hour race in Cleveland.

For the first half of the race, I paced alongside some of the mid-pack ultra runners, who would normally be somewhat slower than my race pace. Today was a much different story. After about five loops, I could not focus properly on my running and I started to fall badly behind everyone. I felt guilty that Mina was at home in recovery mode, and that I took the day to participate in an event that I was not psychologically or physically prepared. Only shear determination allowed me to complete the final five loops, with a finish time of 6:57.

The final two races of the series were a total write-off. The Horror 50-km trail race at the end of October near Kitchener, Ontario saw some really cold and rainy weather, which made the 2.5-km trail loop tricky to negotiate with the muddy conditions. I packed it in after 25-km and consequently did not earn any points. The final event, the Fat Ass 50-km trail race in November saw even worse conditions, with snow and ice covering most of the course. I did only one 10-km loop and surrendered after just about everyone in the race passed me at 5-km.

Even with the non-completion of the final two races, I still had earned enough points to get second place in the 2018 Ontario series. I did not stick around for the awards ceremony, but headed back to Toronto, humbled by life's turn of events that thrust Mina's and my own life into total disarray. However, we both possessed a level of determination that was unshakable, no matter how much adversity we faced from two bouts with cancer.

# 2019 The Ultimate Competitor : Multiple Myeloma

## 雪上加霜: 'One disaster after another'

The 2019 Boston Marathon was the 123rd running of the Boston Athletic Association's Boston Marathon. Lawrence Cherono won the men's foot race in 2:07:57 and Worknesh Degefa won the women's foot race in 2:23.31. My own racing plans were put on hold. Although I did not sign up for any running events in 2019, I continued with running on the indoor YMCA track whenever I had a few hours rest from my role as a caregiver.

Mina's recovery from the oral cancer surgery was progressing nicely. By now, she had graduated to eating solid foods and was planning to return to work in March. We had several clinic appointments with Doctor Jolie Ringash, the Radiation Oncologist at the Princess Margaret Hospital to discuss the role of postoperative radiotherapy for her low-grade mucoepidermoid carcinoma. She said the surgical margins were uninvolved by the invasive tumour and fifteen lymph nodes were resected, none of which was positive for carcinoma.

The doctor indicated that the risk of tumour recurrence is relatively low given the pathological findings. There is opportunity for salvage if the cancer recurs in the future as low grade mucoepidermoid carcinoma tends to grow slowly. As such, observation is a reasonable approach. On the other hand, since the surgery margins were close, postoperative radiotherapy can be considered, to eliminate any residual cancer cells. After reviewing the possible acute and late side effects of radiotherapy, Mina and I decided to go with the observational approach. The last thing we needed was more damage from radiation and another extended recovery period.

There was a possibility that the nerves to Mina's tongue that were severed by the surgery could regenerate over time. However, Mina was still struggling with the speech impediment that resulted from the partial loss of function in her tongue. In January, we booked several appointments with a Speech Language Therapist. The therapist prescribed a series of exaggerated physical exercises involving the mouth and tongue muscles. There was also a prescription for verbal exercises, with over-emphasis of each word. Mina would sit in front of my laptop computer and make video recordings of herself as she recited phrases from books and television shows. I was extremely proud of her determination and resolve to return her body to a state of normal, both physically and emotionally.

During the month of February, 2019, after five months away from work, I received notification from the human resources department that my short-term sick leave allowance had expired. They had provided me the application forms for long-term disability. I certainly did not relish the thought of jumping through hoops trying to negotiate long-term disability with the insurance company.

Since Mina's recovery was proceeding on-track, I decided to return to my work life as a Senior Budget Analyst in the first week of March. We still had follow-up hospital appointments, but my employer was flexible enough to allow me the time off to provide Mina with the required caregiver support.

In the first week of February, before my return to the office, Mina slipped and fell down the basement stairs. Since she landed on her rear-end, there did not seem to be much damage resulting from the fall. Afterwards she did experience some stabbing pain in her ribs. Mina's family doctor ordered blood work and a urine test.

The lab results indicated that there was protein in the urine. There was also follow-up with a bone scan which indicated activity in the left lateral tenth rib and the left anterior eighth rib consistent with probable rib fractures, and there were no other lesions and nothing to suggest the cancer had spread to the bones. The doctors said that they did not think this was related to the low-grade mucoepidermoid oral cavity cancer.

By the first week of March, 2019, I had returned to work on a full-time basis. However, Mina's rib pain did not seem to be resolving itself. In the third week of March, Mina had a CT scan of her chest as well, as her abdomen and pelvis. The lab report did mention an enlargement of a left lower cervical supraclavicular lymph node, just above the collarbone. In the bones there was a new lytic lesion (bone destruction) in the left seventh rib and in the left ninth rib, and a new sclerotic lesion (an unusual thickening of the bone).

In regards to the CT scan of the bones, however, there were new destructive bone lesions in the left inferior pubic ramus (part of the pelvis), left acetabulum (where the pelvis meets the upper end of the thigh bone), left and right iliac crests (part of the hip bone), and right sacral ala (base of the spine) with involvement of the S1 nerve root in the spine.

Before I had returned home from work that day, Mina's family doctor called her to give her the bad news from the lab report. "Based on the CT scan results, it seems that the oral cancer has spread. You will be referred to the cancer specialists at Mount Sinai and Princess Margaret hospitals. Try to be positive and hope for the best." When I arrived home, I noticed that Mina was strangely silent while sitting in her favorite reclining chair. And then she burst into tears and told me about the test results indicating the cancer had spread to her bones. She lamented about the decision not to proceed with the post-surgery radiation therapy for the oral cancer.

This news put me into a state of shock and disbelief. My immediate thoughts were "This is one disaster after another." After regaining my composure, we both discussed this turn of events and vowed to fight this new cancer diagnosis together. We then took our regular evening walk together along the local trail. Previously, our walks together gave us an opportunity to talk about our future retirement plans and exotic places to travel to. Now, the narrative changed

completely to discussions of survival, wills and estate planning.

# Getting Ready for Radiation Therapy

A few days later, we had an appointment with Dr. Monteiro, the surgeon that removed the oral cancer. I asked him "How serious is this new result from the imaging tests?" He indicated that it was a very serious outcome, assuming that the oral cancer had spread to the bones. He then provided a requisition for radiation therapy to begin the next day and continue for several sessions over the next few weeks.

We arrived at the Princess Margaret Cancer Center the next day for the initial appointment with Dr. Hosni, one of the radiation oncologists. There was no radiation treatment scheduled for that day. He was primarily concerned with a specific result of Mina's recent bloodwork, the elevated level of calcium in the blood, termed hypercalcemia. He then left the examination room and we assumed that the appointment was concluded.

Still in the dark, we made our way back home, somewhat perplexed that there was no direction with regards to the next steps. And then we received a frantic telephone call from Dr. Hosni. Apparently, we should not have left the hospital since he wanted us to go immediately to the emergency department to treat the elevated calcium level. He directed us to go to our nearest local hospital emergency department and get treatment for the hypercalcemia (too much calcium in the blood).

This put both of us into a panic mode. We drove to the Humber Regional Hospital, a few miles from our home and checked-in. The emergency department is definitely not one of my favoured options for medical treatment. Not only is the wait time astronomical, there was also the issue of trying to explain Mina's medical history and current condition. I did my best to recite everything I could, strictly from memory. Even when I managed to explain the elevated calcium levels in her blood, we had to wait more than two hours to see a doctor.

They led us to an examination room where a blood draw was taken. A few hours later, the emergency room doctor paid us a visit. She said that the calcium level was indeed elevated but it did not require immediate medical intervention since the level was borderline high. We then were released from the hospital and headed back home.

## We Need to Put the Brakes on This

A few days later, we had a follow-up appointment at the Princess Margaret Cancer Center to discuss the upcoming schedule for Mina's radiation treatments. We met with Dr. Hosni and several radiologists. Given Mina's history of head and neck cancer, it initially was felt that this represented metastatic disease, where the low-grade oral cancer had spread. If this were the case, the prognosis would be extremely grim. However, since this was a low-grade mucoepidermoid carcinoma of the floor of mouth, although not impossible, it would be extremely rare for this type of cancer to spread.

After a short consultation, the doctors said "At this point, we need to put the brakes on proceeding with radiation therapy. We believe that you may have a new cancer, multiple myeloma. We need to refer you to a specialist in the hematology department to confirm the diagnosis. The treatment for multiple myeloma would be totally different. You also have an enlarged lymph node which requires a biopsy." We were both dumfounded that this may be a new cancer. Moreover, we did not have a clue as to what multiple myeloma was, having never heard of it before.

The next day, we had a follow-up appointment with Dr. Monteiro, the surgeon who removed the tumour from Mina's mouth. We advised him of the possible multiple myeloma diagnosis. He remarked, "Multiple myeloma? You can go fifteen or twenty years with that disease, with the appropriate treatment." That gave us somewhat of a glimmer of hope.

I still wanted to know if there was any relationship to the oral cancer. Apparently, it was just coincidental that a new, unrelated cancer had emerged. Dr. Monteiro said, "This is just really bad luck." With that, Dr. Monteiro performed a fine needle biopsy on an enlarged lymph node in Mina's neck. Thankfully, the lab report indicated no spread of the oral cavity cancer.

## Tests, Tests and More Tests

Radiation therapy was not pursued for the bone lesion in Mina's spine. The report from the radiation oncologists provided a schedule for 'Blood work with a CBC, calcium, albumin, and creatinine as well as SPEP and UPEP tests.' Since this medical terminology was completely foreign to me, I had to research each of the terms using 'Dr. Google.' I was more at ease with Chinese language learning!

From our previous encounter with Dr. Hosni, I was familiar with the term 'calcium' but was unsure how the measurement of calcium had any relevance. He explained that calcium is the most common mineral in the body. If there is an elevated level of calcium in the body tissues, it could be life-threatening.

## Albumin and Creatinine

Albumin and creatinine were completely new words that required translation into plain English. The oncologists stated that they needed to measure the amount of albumin in Mina's blood. Low albumin levels can indicate a problem with her liver or kidneys. They also needed to measure Mina's creatinine by getting a urine and a blood sample in order to monitor her kidney function.

Normally, the kidneys filter creatinine from your blood and send it out of the body in your urine. If there is a problem with your kidneys, creatinine can build up in the blood and less will be released in urine. If blood and/or urine creatinine levels are not normal, it can be a sign of kidney disease. Since Mina also had diabetes, her family doctor had indicated that she was at higher risk for kidney disease.

## The SPEP Test

The SPEP test refers to Serum Protein Electrophoresis. This lab test measures the quantity of proteins in the fluid (serum) part of a blood sample. The results of the SPEP test pinpointed the problem. The doctors explained that there should only be the albumin spike showing up on the graph if there is no disease present. However, Mina's graph clearly showed a second spike, which represented the additional proteins.

The doctors informed us that the second spike indicated a monoclonal protein, called an M-spike. This was really bad news since this type of protein is found in unusually large amounts in the blood or urine of people with multiple myeloma and other types of plasma cell tumours.

## The UPEP Test

UPEP is defined as Urine Protein Electrophoresis. The urine protein electrophoresis test is used to estimate how much of certain proteins are in the urine. Normally there is no protein, or only a small amount of protein in the urine. Similar to the SPEP test, the UPEP also detects albumin and any abnormal proteins.

We were informed that an abnormally high amount of protein in the urine can be a sign of many different disorders, including inflammation, kidney problems, and multiple myeloma. Mina's urine test result also indicated an abnormal level of proteins in the urine. The tests were all pointing in the same direction, confirming our worst fears, a diagnosis of multiple myeloma.

## Immunofixation Electrophoresis (IFE) Test

The doctors had also ordered another test called immunofixation electrophoresis (IFE), which completely confounded me. Again, I was forced to do some internet research to determine the meaning behind this test. This is defined as a specialized type of test that can identify the exact type of abnormal protein that makes up the M-spike, the sharp second spike pattern on Mina's graph.

# Keeping up with Bence-Jones

The immunologist interpreted Mina's test results as Bence-Jones protein, lambda. This was one of the abnormal proteins that had an extremely high abnormal value of 2,489 mg per litre, where the normal range should be between 5.7 and 26.3. The report also indicated elevated creatinine and calcium levels, along with low hemoglobin (a protein in the red blood cells that carries oxygen) and high white blood cells (immune system cells that protect the body against infections).

I looked up the definition of Bence-Jones protein. It is a small protein made by the cancerous myeloma plasma cell. It is found in the urine of most people with multiple myeloma. Bence-Jones proteins consist of either kappa or lambda light chain types. Bence-Jones proteins are small enough to be filtered out by the kidneys. The proteins then spill into the urine.

A normal result would show very few of these proteins present in the urine. But Mina's urine test result was abnormal, showing Bence-Jones lambda protein, associated with an abnormal IgD monoclonal protein, an extremely rare sub-type of multiple myeloma.

## Major Bone Damage

Additional findings from the lab reports and imaging scans were also concerning. In the skull there are multiple lytic lesions (holes in the bone) throughout the calvarium (a portion of the skull including the braincase). The holes varied in size, the largest being approximately 1 cm. In the spine there were degenerative disc changes, but no definite bone lesions. In the pelvis and femurs, there were bone lesions within both femurs (the long bones located in the thigh). There were no definite bone lesions within the ribs, but there were multiple lesions within the clavicle (collarbone) and scapula (shoulder bone). There were multiple lesions in the humeri (the bones of the upper arm or forelimb, forming joints at the shoulder and the elbow).

## The Race Against Multiple Myeloma

After weeding through all of the medical terminology in the lab reports, we began to get a clearer idea of what we were dealing with – a fairly rare and incurable form of blood cancer, multiple myeloma. This presented us with a different level of competitor than we had dealt with before. We successfully defeated the papillary thyroid cancer that invaded Mina's body in 2001. The salivary gland cancer, although much more challenging, was beaten back through aggressive surgery in 2018.

Conquering multiple myeloma would be analogous to myself, an amateur runner, lining up at the start line of the Boston Marathon, hoping to outrun all of the elite runners. It seemed like a futile effort, knowing that this was an incurable disease, with many potentially nasty complications. Psychologically, Mina and I were both devastated with this outcome. We prayed and remained hopeful, as we prepared for our first meeting with the cancer doctors at the Princess Margaret Hospital.

## Meet the Multiple Myeloma Experts

Dr. Hosni, the radiation oncologist, referred us to the Myeloma Clinic at the Princess Margaret Hospital to be under the care of Dr. Donna Reece, a respected hematologist and researcher in the field of multiple myeloma. Our first appointment was on April 19, 2019 where Dr. Hyra Sapru, an associate of Dr. Reece, reviewed Mina's clinical history and the test results conducted by Dr. Hosni.

At this point, Mina was experiencing significant pain in her right hip and was limping when she walked. The pain radiated from her groin into the right leg. She was forced to use a walking cane to assist with her mobility. She often awoke during the middle of the night and was using hydromorphone daily to alleviate the pain. She had ongoing lower back pain and a new pain developed in her right ribs. Whenever she coughed, this intensified the pain level. Mina had finally recovered from the shingles infection, which took over six months to resolve. But she was experiencing extreme shortness of breath whenever she undertook the slightest level of exertion, such as going for a short walk. Of special concern was the frothy urine she had been excreting since the beginning of 2019.

After reviewing the initial lab results, Dr. Sapru's first impression was that the results were certainly suspicious of multiple myeloma, mostly due to the extensive lesions in the skeletal bones, anemia, high calcium levels, mild kidney impairment, elevated Beta-2 micro-globulin and the Bence-Jones proteins found in the urine.

# The Bone Marrow Biopsy

The next step was to perform a bone marrow biopsy. Mina was instructed to lay on her side while the doctor inserted a biopsy needle into the hip bone. The results were not promising since a proper bone marrow sample could not be obtained. Multiple attempts were made, however, only to produce a dry tap which was absolutely useless and could not be sent to the lab for diagnosis. The doctor finally ended up snipping a small bone fragment from Mina's hip which was sent for analysis. After all the pain Mina endured from this procedure, it was disappointing to learn that genetic testing on the sample would not be possible.

Despite the issue with the bone marrow sample, the doctors were ninety-percent certain of the multiple myeloma diagnosis, given the elevated levels of protein in the urine and the rapid onset of the symptoms. They told us that the myeloma was likely at an advanced stage. The symptoms were also consistent with a high-risk, aggressive sub-type of multiple myeloma.

Although it is presently an incurable disease, there are treatment options that could put the cancer into remission. I requested a prognosis, but could not get a definitive response. Apparently, it is not a one-size-fits-all type of cancer. It has many different variations with survival rates that depend upon a host of different factors such as patient age, co-morbidities (diabetes, high blood pressure) and genetic factors.

This left Mina and I completely speechless, combined with an utter sense of hopelessness. Having zero knowledge of this rare blood cancer made it next to impossible to mentally process the diagnosis we were handed. After out-running the thyroid and salivary gland cancers, this was similar to hitting the wall and crashing at 20 miles of a 26.2-mile marathon.

## Sometimes the Cure is Worse Than the Disease

As we were absorbing this news, the doctors discussed the next steps. They still needed to get the bone marrow biopsy results to confirm the diagnosis. Although there was no viable bone marrow sample, some analysis could be done on the bone chip that was extracted. The plan was to start chemotherapy within two weeks.

Prior to the upcoming chemo treatments, Mina was prescribed a daily dose of dexamethasone, a common steroid drug that treats inflammation. Since this drug increases blood sugar, we were advised to monitor Mina's blood sugar on a daily basis. She was already taking Metformin to control her type-II diabetes, but the dose had to now be doubled to offset the side-effects of the dexamethasone.

Later on, I would learn and come to accept the fact that the side-effects from drug therapies used to treat the symptoms can be worse than the actual disease itself. As a long-distance runner, I was already accustomed to this reality. If your muscles feel like hell halfway through a marathon race, just pop a few extra strength Ibuprofen, relieve the muscle pain and end up puking your guts out from the stomach irritation as you cross the finish line.

## A Bucket Full of Urine

Finally, we were given a huge container to take home with us to collect a 24-hour urine sample to quantify the amount of protein in the urine. At the time, I had no idea how a urine sample could provide useful information into Mina's diagnosis. All I could recall from Dr. Hosni's initial urine analysis was the term Bence-Jones protein, with lambda light-chain.

Clearly, this disease was a lot more complicated than we expected. I made it my mission to do some extensive internet searches to get myself educated as quickly as possible. As soon as I returned home, I downloaded the Multiple Myeloma Patient Handbook from the Myeloma Canada website. This turned out to be an invaluable resource which prepared us for our next meeting with the myeloma experts.

## Confirming the Diagnosis

We had the follow-up appointment with the hematology doctors on April 25, 2019. Mina was limping badly and using a walking cane for mobility. She was still suffering from the painful bone marrow biopsy that was performed at the previous appointment. Dr. Sapru and Dr. Reece met with us to confirm the results of the latest medical tests. They indicated that the bone marrow was 90% packed with myeloma plasma cells. Although the genetic testing could not be performed, the rapid onset of the disease and symptoms, indicated a high-risk form of multiple myeloma that required immediate intervention.

After hearing this news, Mina just looked at me with tears in her eyes, waving her hand and uttering "bye-bye." Of course, I did not want to hear this. Either I was an internal optimist, pinning my hopes that medical science would eventually prevail or I was in a state of total denial. All other kinds of emotions and feelings flooded my brain, including panic, anxiety and confusion. I had already taken some Ativan, an anti-anxiety drug that my family doctor prescribed, but it did not seem to be very effective.

# Testing My Knowledge

The first thing the doctors asked us was "What do you know about multiple myeloma?" This caught me a bit off-guard but at the same time seemed to kick-start my mental functioning. It signalled that the doctors were really interested in having the patients actively involved in the discussion and decision-making. When one is forced to focus their thoughts on science, and not be clouded in a sea of emotion, this has a calming effect. It is similar to running into a bad patch in a tough ultra running event. I had learned from other runners to try mental tricks such as counting odd numbers up to '77' and then back down to '1', repeating as needed. These psychological maneuvers really do work to eliminate the physical distress from running countless miles.

I suppose the doctors were also testing my knowledge to assess how effective I could be as a patient advocate and caregiver. From my very brief review of the Multiple Myeloma Patient Handbook and the internet searches, all that I could recall were the different stages of multiple myeloma. I replied with an uncertain degree of confidence, "This is a fairly rare type of blood cancer. There are various stages involved in this disease. The first stage is MGUS or Monoclonal Gammopathy of Undetermined Significance."

This new medical terminology was a mouthful for me and I struggled to pronounce it accurately. The doctors expressed surprise that I actually could reference this term. "Basically, the MGUS stage shows an increased level of an abnormal protein, but no other myeloma disease symptoms are present. A patient would not require therapy for this stage, but careful on-going monitoring would be needed to see if it progresses to a more active stage. The risk of the disease progressing into myeloma is about 1% per year." I was astounded by how information much I could actually regurgitate from the Dr. Google research I had conducted.

I continued with my pseudo-medical rant about the other stages of multiple myeloma, but really struggled with recalling any useful details. I could only reply in a very general sense and said, "The next stage is called smoldering myeloma, which indicates that the disease has progressed through the presentation of additional symptoms. For example, there may be an increase in the protein levels, anemia and high calcium in the blood. Finally, there would be stages I, II and III, which indicate different levels of active myeloma."

# The CRAB Criteria

After listening to my layperson's explanation, the hematologists went into a more fulsome description of the disease and potential treatment options. They said, "This is a cancer of the plasma cells. These cells, when healthy, produce proteins called immunoglobulins (IgG, IgA, IgM, IgE and IgD) that fight infections. These proteins consist of a heavy chain, combined with a light chain component, either a kappa or lambda light chain."

However, a cancerous plasma cell will produce a rogue immunoglobulin, called a monoclonal protein, which is a defective immunoglobulin. Monoclonal proteins cannot defend against infections and they crowd out all of the healthy red and white blood cells in your bone marrow. The cancer cells also spit out an abundance of free light chains, either the kappa or lambda light chains, which are not attached to the heavy chains and basically clog up the kidneys. Mina's diagnosis was explained as multiple myeloma consisting of an IgD monoclonal protein with a free light chain lambda.

"The disease also has other nasty side-effects such as holes in the bones, high calcium blood levels, kidney damage and anemia. Your wife has the classic CRAB symptoms which are strongly associated with a diagnosis of multiple myeloma. For this type of cancer, there is no cure but we can provide therapies that will slow the disease progression and improve quality of life. Don't worry, we will get you back to feeling more like your old self again. Before we get into the latest lab test results, do you have any questions?"

If you find yourself in this position as a myeloma patient caregiver, being a layperson, this diagnostic information will seem to overwhelming and difficult to digest. The only question that I could come up with at the time was "What the heck does CRAB mean?"

The doctors then explained, "CRAB is just a short-form that we use. The 'C' indicates high calcium levels in the blood. The 'R' stands for a compromised renal (kidney) function. The 'A' refers to anemia, which results in low oxygen delivery to the body cells, causing feelings of fatigue. Finally, the 'B' is short-form for bone disease, where the myeloma has punched holes (lytic lesions) primarily in the skull, hips and ribs."

## What is the Prognosis?

I was anxious to get an idea of how advanced Mina's myeloma was in terms of disease stage and I asked them, "Exactly what stage are we dealing with and what is the prognosis?" The response confirmed my worst fears. "Unfortunately, the cancer is at stage III, which is the terminal stage. Most people get diagnosed at this late stage since the early symptoms of bone pain and fatigue usually get attributed to the normal process of aging, such as arthritis. It is what it is."

The doctors could not provide a prognosis since myeloma is such a complex disease. The prognosis would depend on various factors such as high-risk genetic mutations, patient age, the disease stage at diagnosis and response to treatment.

## Navigating the Lab Test Results Maze

We then proceeded to discuss the latest lab test results from the blood draw. The lab results were illustrated in a simple, easy-to-understand graphical format, which showed where the normal range should be compared with Mina's actual results. Any abnormal readings were flagged in a bright orange colour. Prior to the appointment, I had some time to look at the results. I was totally confused by most of the technical medical terminology and consequently had to conduct endless hours of internet searches to find out what the results represented.

## Lactate Dehydrogenase (LDH)

The first abnormal orange test result that caught my attention was related to LDH (Lactate Dehydrogenase). The doctors said that LDH is an enzyme, found in almost every body cell, that helps produce energy in the body. The test is used to measure low red blood cells and different types of blood cancer. Elevated levels are a sure sign of major inflammation.

Mina's LDH was measured at 436 micro-moles per litre, well above the upper normal limit of 220. The doctors explained that elevated LDH levels can be caused by many different factors, including multiple myeloma.

## The Complete Blood Count (CBC)

Mina's complete blood count showed an abnormally low value of 115 grams per litre for the hemoglobin. No wonder she was constantly fatigued. There was an insufficient amount of oxygen being delivered to her system, a classic sign of anemia. As a runner, I understood the importance of maintaining a healthy hemoglobin value. Runners need a stable supply of oxygen flow to the cardio-vascular system, otherwise we crash and burn in a fast-paced race.

The white blood count (WBC), the cells that fight infections, was also abnormal and quite elevated at 14.1. This may be due to any number of reasons, including, various blood cancers, specific drugs such as steroids and inflammatory diseases.

## Abnormal Immunoglobulins

As the doctors previously explained to us, the immunoglobulins are groups of proteins produced by the immune system by the plasma cells in the bone marrow in order to fight different types of infections.

The results from Mina's immunoglobulin blood test were concerning. The IgG value was low at 5.4 grams per litre, where this should be between 7.0 and 16.0. The IgA value was extremely low at 0.08 grams per litre whereas the normal values should be between 0.7 and 4.0. The doctors advised that these abnormal results were not surprising, given how the cancerous myeloma plasma cells multiply rapidly and crowd out the bone marrow, which reduces the healthy immunoglobulins in the immune system.

### The Free Light Chain Test : A Key Marker of Myeloma

Of critical importance was the blood serum free light chain test. This measures the amount of Bence-Jones protein for both the kappa and lambda light chain values. The normal lambda light chain value should be from 5.7 mg per litre to 26.3 mg per litre. The test conducted on the previous test on April 19th showed a Bence-Jones protein, lambda of 2,489 mg per litre.

The free lambda on the current test also reflected an abnormal value of 1,854 mg/L. The current result, although still abnormal, showed a significant reduction. The doctors said this was an excellent response and was solely attributed to the dexamethasone steroid pills that Mina had taken. This gave us hope that further intense chemotherapy, using the latest drug cocktails, could result in a more robust response to get the myeloma under control.

## Creatinine and Kidney Function

The creatinine test results showed an abnormally high value of 127 umol/L which was even more elevated from the April 19th value of 101 (the normal range is from 50 to 98). This was an ominous sign of kidney function impairment, probably as a result of the myeloma combined with Mina's type II diabetes.

Associated with this test was the estimated glomerular kidney filtration rate (eGFR), measured at 50 milliliters per minute on April 19th and falling to 38 ml/minute on the current test. The normal rate of kidney filtration should be at least 60 ml/minute. The doctors recommended boosting Mina's daily water intake to get the kidney function back to the normal filtration rate.

# Beta-2-Microglobulin Test

The Beta-2-microglobulin is defined as a small protein normally found on the surface of many cells in small amounts in the blood and urine. An increased amount in the blood or urine may be a sign of certain diseases, including some types of cancer, such as multiple myeloma or lymphoma.

Tumour markers such as the Beta-2-microglobulin are substances made by cancer cells or by normal cells in response to cancer within the body. Mina's beta-2-microglobulin was measured at 6.7 mg per litre. The normal range is from 0.6 to 2.3. The doctors explained that this was one of the key measures, along with the high LDH level, which was used to determine that the myeloma was at stage III. They would also use this test to monitor the progress of the disease to determine if there is a relapse after Mina's treatment program.

## The Monoclonal Protein Test

The monoclonal protein IgD (the defective immunoglobulin produced by the cancerous plasma cells) level obtained was 4,361 g/L (the normal level is 8 to 132). The doctors planned to repeat the serum protein electrophoresis (SPEP) and immunofixation electrophoresis (IFE) tests periodically during the course of treatment. However, they planned to rely primarily on the free light chain test to measure the light chain lambda levels to evaluate how well Mina was responding to therapy.

# Viral Testing

As we were made aware of, multiple myeloma compromises the immune system by crowding out the healthy red and white blood cells in the bone marrow. White blood cells, which include the immunoglobulins, are an essential component of the immune system that fight bacterial and viral infections. If you don't have the optimal level of healthy antibodies, the risk of infection poses a serious threat.

As a result of her weakened immune system from multiple myeloma, Mina experienced an outbreak of the shingles virus after the oral cancer surgery. Shingles is an outbreak of rash or blisters on the skin. Shingles is caused by the varicella-zoster virus - the same virus that causes chickenpox. After you have chickenpox, the virus stays in your body.

This may not cause problems for many years. But as you get older, the virus may reappear as shingles, which happened in Mina's case. To prevent against future outbreaks, Mina was prescribed an antiviral medication called acyclovir. She was advised to take a 400 mg tablet twice a day, basically forever.

Acyclovir is a type of anti-viral medication. It prevents different types of viral infections when your body has a weak immune system. It works by stopping the spread of the herpes zoster virus in the body. I later learned that an acyclovir prescription is quite standard for myeloma patients as a preventative measure against shingles re-activation. Since Mina never had a shingles vaccination, the acyclovir medication was of critical importance.

Mina also tested positive for past exposure to the Hepatitis B virus. Hepatitis is an inflammation of the liver. Fortunately, there is a vaccine for hepatitis B. It requires three shots. However, Mina had never previously received this vaccination. It was quite possible that she had been exposed to the virus long ago when she was in the Philippines.

We were referred to Dr. Cunningham, a hepatologist, at the Toronto General Hospital who, by definition, specialized in liver function. Mina was prescribed Entecavir, a 0.5 mg dose to be taken every other day. Entecavir is used to treat chronic (long-term) hepatitis B infections (swelling of the liver caused by a virus). The potential side-effects are nausea and headaches. The drug could also hurt the kidneys. Mina's kidney function would be monitored monthly to ensure the kidney filtration rate would stay within an acceptable range.

# Let Confucius Be Your Guide

## 三人行，必有我師

"Amongst three people walking, any one of them can be my teacher"

- Confucius

There is a famous saying from the ancient Chinese philosopher Confucius: 'Amongst three people walking, any one of them can be my teacher.' Confucius is widely considered as one of the most important and influential individuals in human history. His teaching and philosophy greatly impacted people around the world and remain influential today. His moral teachings emphasized self-cultivation, pursuit of self-improvement, and the attainment of skilled judgment rather than knowledge of rules. In short, when discussing multiple myeloma with your medical team, you must take responsibility for cultivating your own knowledge.

Other people have knowledge that you may lack. You will definitely be relying on the medical experts to provide guidance throughout the multiple myeloma journey. However, you do not have to be a passive participant in this process, no matter how complicated the journey may seem. Active involvement relates to knowledge-sharing, treatment decisions, and the management of the side-effects of treatment.

It is your responsibility to listen, learn and make your own contribution to the discussion with the medical team. This is where your role as a patient advocate becomes critical. Communication is a two-way street. Don't hesitate to ask questions and even get a second opinion if needed. However, if you want to be content with just listening and following the rules as recommended by your doctors, that option is perfectly fine too.

Keep in mind that active involvement may result in a superior outcome for your loved one. With multiple myeloma, there is not a rigidly defined set of rules with respect to therapy. Each patient's disease progression, response to treatment and outcome is unique.

The prescribed drug treatment program for multiple myeloma will be based on years of clinical trials and peer-reviewed scientific studies that validate the safety and effectiveness of each drug or combination of drugs. The onus is on you, the patient advocate and caregiver to review the scientific data pertaining to any drug treatment program that is prescribed by your medical team. You don't have to necessarily read the research papers to gain an understanding of the proposed therapy.

There are many useful webinars and on-line video resources that are geared to explaining the different options in layperson's terms. There is not a one-size-fits-all therapy. Even the most experienced and respected hematologists will disagree to a certain degree on which drug combinations to use and also how to manage the side-effects of treatment. You will discover that treatment decisions can be more of an art than a science.

Although I am a self-coached runner, the training programs that I adhered to were based on the principles of science and physiology. I did not simply awake one morning, lace up some running shoes and head outside for a run. There were running gurus and experts who had much more in-depth knowledge on the subject than I did. I purchased books on everything from beginners running to advanced competitive running. I followed guidance on the type of running shoe to wear based on my own running physiology and biomechanics.

I eventually joined a Thursday evening run club which had professional coaches giving advice on how to do proper speedwork to improve one's running performance. I did not blindly follow the prescribed training programs, but rather tweaked the program to match my own circumstances. In the end, I consciously modified Confucius' idiom to 'Amongst three people running, all of them can be my teacher.'

# Getting Control of Myeloma : Induction Therapy

Moving forward, the medical team provided recommendations on the first stage of the multiple myeloma treatment program, called 'induction.' The plan was to start CYBOR-D, a triplet drug chemotherapy, the following week.

The 'C' is short-form for cyclophosphamide. The doctors advised that cyclophosphamide is a type of agent that damages the cell's DNA and may kill cancer cells. It may also lower the body's immune response.

The 'BOR' is short-form for Bortezomib (Velcade). Bortezomib is a drug which blocks several molecular pathways in a cell and may cause cancer cells to die. It is a type of proteasome inhibitor which blocks the action of proteasomes. A proteasome is a large protein complex that helps destroy other cellular proteins when they are no longer needed. If the proteasome is blocked, the proteins cannot escape, which causes the proteins to build-up and kill the cancer cell.

The 'D' is short-form for Dexamethasone. This is a steroid drug used to reduce inflammation and lower the body's immune response. It is used with other drugs to treat many different types of cancer, including multiple myeloma. Dexamethasone and the other steroids are useful in myeloma treatment because they can stop white blood cells from traveling to areas where cancerous myeloma cells are causing damage.

# The Steroid Curse

However, steroids are a double-edged sword. They can give you a huge energy boost, but then increase blood sugar and make you prone to irrational mood swings. Once the drug leaves your system, it can result in a crash. Our medical team indicated that, despite the negative side effects of steroids, the benefits outweigh the costs, especially if it is combined with the other myeloma drugs.

As a patient care-giver, I witnessed first-hand the side effects of dexamethasone. After taking her dexamethasone cocktail, Mina asked me to go outside in the garden and do some weeding. Even at the best of times, I am not 'Mr. Home Handyman.' Everything that I touch tends to result in a complete disaster. This principle seems to apply even to the simplest of tasks, such as gardening.

I proceeded with surgical precision to dig up all of those nasty weeds covering the front yard garden, giving myself kudos in the process. The only problem was that the 'weeds' I was digging up were actually the beautiful ground cover foliage that Mina had carefully cultivated when she was healthy. When Mina reviewed my gardening project, she immediately burst out into hysterics. I wanted to crawl under the nearest garden rock to escape the resulting dexamethasone storm!

We were provided information regarding this type of chemotherapy, in addition to managing the side effects of chemotherapy. The side effects of CYBOR-D include nausea and myelosuppression (decreased red and white blood cells in the bone marrow) associated with the chemo drug cyclophosphamide, along with peripheral neuropathy (nerve damage that causes numbness in the hands and feet), and diarrhea. Viral reactivation, especially related to shingles,

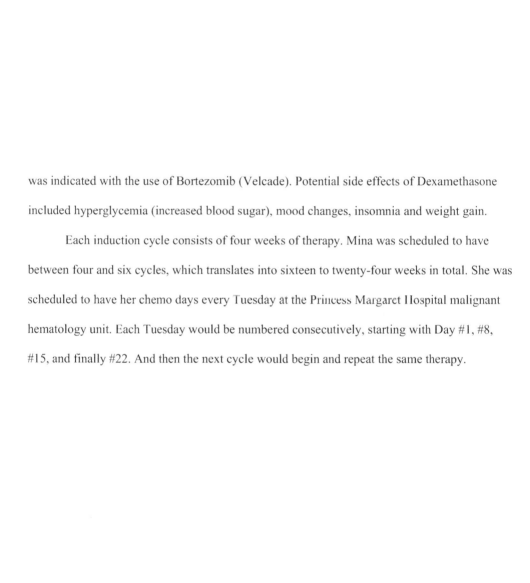

was indicated with the use of Bortezomib (Velcade). Potential side effects of Dexamethasone included hyperglycemia (increased blood sugar), mood changes, insomnia and weight gain.

Each induction cycle consists of four weeks of therapy. Mina was scheduled to have between four and six cycles, which translates into sixteen to twenty-four weeks in total. She was scheduled to have her chemo days every Tuesday at the Princess Margaret Hospital malignant hematology unit. Each Tuesday would be numbered consecutively, starting with Day #1, #8, #15, and finally #22. And then the next cycle would begin and repeat the same therapy.

# The Daily Medical Journal

At this point, I realized that I would be completely overwhelmed if I did not set up a game plan and get organized. Mina was consuming several different types of medications in addition to the CYBOR-D chemo treatments. I decided to drop by the local bookstore to purchase a daily diary in which I could record everything, including;

- Scheduled appointments (time, location, specialist name)
- List of medications, dosages and time of day administered
- Vitals such as blood pressure, body temperature and glucose levels
- List of symptoms and pain levels
- Comments and directions indicated by the doctors and nurse practitioners
- Key results from lab reports and clinic notes
- Key contacts, including business cards of the medical team and our local pharmacy

Why go to the trouble of recording this level of detail every day? You will soon realize that this routine is absolutely worth its weight in gold. Multiple myeloma is a complex disease. It is quite difficult, even for trained medical professionals, to distinguish symptoms which are the result of the disease, the prescribed medications or other co-morbidities that the patient has.

Similar to a runner's GPS watch, accurate record-keeping provides a roadmap of where the patient has been and how much progress the patient is achieving. Runners know that a training program is only as good as the activities which are carefully measured over time and then evaluated as to the degree of success achieved.

Similarly, a multiple myeloma training log will provide valuable information on initial baseline data at diagnosis which can be compared with the results of the treatment program. The caregiver has information right at their fingertips which can be informative in terms of providing helpful guidance to the medical team. The doctors do have access to all of the test results on their respective hospital databases. However, this data limited to a point-in-time and the longer-term trends. It cannot capture the day-to-day nuances and subjective feelings of the patient.

# An Appointment to Remember

On-going hospital appointments and myeloma clinic visits will become a permanent way of life for all patients and their caregivers. More often than not, the different specialists will be working out of different hospitals. The blood testing laboratories, imaging centres and dental clinics will also be located in various buildings and floors. Even if you use the internet to map out the route to the hospital and the exact location within the building, the odds of you being able to remember this detail upon arrival at the hospital are improbable.

At the very top of the daily diary, it is imperative to write down the hospital name, specific unit, floor location, the name of your doctor and the scheduled time of your appointment. This will save you valuable time and effort when you arrive for the hospital visit. You will not need to track down a busy hospital staffer to request directions. You and your loved one will have enough on your minds without having the added pressure of losing your way and possibly missing your appointment.

Upon arrival, ensure that you are familiar with the check-in procedures, as these will differ from facility to facility. Some clinics require that you perform your own weigh-in and record some of your patient's vitals via an electronic portal. Always touch base with the clinic reception area to confirm your appointment and the check-in procedures. Based on my experience, there are instances where a clerical screw-up occurred and the appointment or a critical blood test was not registered in the system.

Keep your daily diary and a pen handy. During the appointment itself, it is useful to record the names of the specialists who meet with you and a brief summary of what was discussed. Jot down any key vital statistics such as blood pressure, pulse rate, body temperature and oxygen saturation levels. You should also provide the medical team with any symptoms experienced by the patient over the past few weeks leading up to the appointment.

## A Prescription for Success

The first thing the doctors will ask is for a list of current medications and dosages. How many of us can really remember drug names (both the scientific and trade names), as well as the specific dosages, side-effects and time of day the drugs were taken? And it is not just one doctor asking the question, but a whole medical team, including nephrologists, pharmacists, endocrinologists, cardiologists, family doctors, dentists and nurse practitioners. At each monthly appointment, we reviewed the entire list again with the same professionals. A daily log will enable you to easily track changes to the prescriptions as well as the addition of new drugs or the deletion of existing ones.

## The Patient Portal

The hospital network offered an extremely useful patient portal. All laboratory test results and clinic visit notes could be accessed via a tablet or laptop computer. When Mina had her blood tests completed, within one hour, I would get an email notification that the results were ready to view. I could then sign-in to the portal to get instant access. The key lab test results could now be recorded in the daily diary prior to the meeting with the hematologists. At a glance, the results indicated the typical normal range. There would be a flag for any results that were abnormal.

As a novice user of the system, at first, the test results had little meaning to me the layperson. All I could do was scratch my head and hope for an interpretation from the doctors that made sense. This is where a little investment in basic google research paid big dividends. While the internet is a valuable tool to assist in the understanding of the disease, diagnosis and treatment programs, caution must be exercised in using Dr. Google.

## Scientific Research Papers

Be aware that peer-reviewed scientific articles presenting the results of clinical trials, will often point to prognostic conclusions for certain genetic sub-types of myeloma that may be alarming to you, the caregiver. Don't accept conclusions in scientific studies as facts. They are pieces of a much larger puzzle that build upon each other to point researchers to more promising areas. This is why myeloma patients are seeing an exponential growth of new drugs and therapies. All of the money poured into research has a big impact over time.

Scientific studies, even those published in prestigious medical journals, can sometimes be unintentionally loaded with different types of biases. The conclusions in one research study or even multiple studies must be taken with a grain of salt. Clinical trials and medical research take slices of a population sample and randomly assign participants to either the group receiving the new therapy or the placebo control group. The sample size may not be sufficient or the design of the study may have inherent errors. Be cautious of clinical trials funded by the big pharmaceutical companies. Although researchers are careful to declare their funding sources and potential conflicts of interest, unintended bias can influence the results.

## The First Four Months : Steady Progress

The first session of induction chemotherapy was scheduled on April 30, 2019 at the Princess Margaret Cancer Centre. Mina had an excellent response with the prior treatment with just the dexamethasone pills which reduced the light chain Bence-Jones lambda protein by a whopping 600 points.

We had even greater expectations for more progress once the induction chemotherapy starts. Moreover, the recent blood test results indicated only a trivial amount of the IgD monoclonal protein from the SPEP and immunofixation tests. However, Mina's kidney function was still impaired with a glomerular filtration rate of 48 millilitres per minute (normal should be at least 60 ml/min.) and a creatinine level of 106, where the normal value should be between 50 and 98.

Her hemoglobin was also abnormally low at 111 grams per litre, which accounted for her symptoms of extreme fatigue due to insufficient oxygen delivery to her system. The blood sugar level was quite elevated as a result of the dexamethasone. The impact of the bone marrow biopsy from the previous week continued to cause her much pain and distress. She could not walk unassisted and needed a cane for support.

It turned out to be a very long and exhausting day for both of us. Mina started the day at 7:00 a.m. with five tablets of dexamethasone. It was then a fifteen-kilometre drive to the hospital and a 9:00 a.m. consultation with one of the hematologists who reviewed the blood test results and the weekly chemotherapy procedures.

## Waiting for Chemotherapy

We then arrived at the 4<sup>th</sup> floor chemotherapy unit to register for the procedure which had been scheduled for 2:00 p.m. They gave Mina a hospital wristband and a pager which would beep when a chair in the chemo unit became available. The waiting area was jammed packed with patients awaiting their treatment for their specific type of blood cancer. The beepers would be sounding off on a regular basis. People would get up when their beeper buzzed, look around the room as if to say "Hey, I just won the chemo lottery, my turn is next!" This could have been a scene directly from a Seinfeld episode!

Mina and I sat in the waiting room for hours, waiting for our beeper to summon us. Eventually, as closing time arrived, the room became empty and it was just Mina and I sitting there, somewhat dazed and confused, wondering why our time had not come. By 4 p.m., one of the chemo nurses walked into the waiting area and called out Mina's name. They were wondering why we had not shown up for our scheduled appointment.

As it turned out, we had been given a faulty pager which malfunctioned and did not alert us. I made a mental note to myself to check back on a regular basis with the reception desk the next time we had a chemo appointment. I was determined not to be thwarted by faulty technology again!

## Our Nurse Practitioner

Eventually, we made it into the malignant hematology unit to start the chemo treatment. We were introduced to Suzanne Rowland, one of the experienced Nurse Practitioners. Her role was to provide support for all of the symptoms of the disease and side-effects of the treatment. This ranged from monitoring for possible infections to providing advice on pain management.

Suzanne's supportive care function would turn out to be invaluable. She was an extremely strong advocate for listening to both the patient and the patient caregiver's needs. If opioid drugs such as hydromorphone were required for pain management, she would not hesitate to prescribe them. Cancer patients have special needs and should not be stigmatized for the use of pain-management drugs.

# Nausea Prevention

Prior to the actual chemo treatment, Mina had to take two Ondansetron tablets to help prevent treatment related nausea. Ondansetron (Zofran) is a drug used to prevent nausea and vomiting caused by chemotherapy and radiation therapy. It is also used to prevent nausea and vomiting after surgery. Ondansetron hydrochloride blocks the action of the chemical serotonin, which may help lessen nausea and vomiting.

The next step involved the sub-cutaneous injection of Bortezomib (Velcade) into the abdomen. This drug is a proteosome inhibitor that blocks several molecular pathways in the cancer cell, causing the cancer cell to die. I made a notation in my diary to indicate that the injection site was located on the right-hand side. It was important to keep a record of the infusion site locations. Mina would be having the same procedure next week and we wanted to avoid continuous trauma to one side of the body. Choosing alternate locations on the abdomen each week seemed like a good strategy.

After the Bortezomib infusion, Mina swallowed seven Cyclophosphamide (Cytoxan) tablets. Cyclophosphamide is in a class of medications called alkylating agents. When cyclophosphamide is used to treat cancer, it works by slowing or stopping the growth of cancer cells in the body. Along with Bortezomib, it can cause nausea or vomiting. Hence the reason Mina had to take the Ondansetron two hours prior to the chemotherapy.

## Bone Strengthening Therapy

The bone lesions (holes) are a major source of concern for myeloma patients. Left untreated, this could lead to serious fractures and spinal injuries. The doctors discussed the possible use of bisphosphonate (bone-strengthening) drugs to help offset the bone damage that the cancer had caused. The plan was to use zoledronic acid (Zometa). This drug would be given by IV (intravenous transfusion) on a monthly basis. However, a nasty potential side-effect of this medication is osteonecrosis of the jaw, where the jaw bone basically dies after something as simple as a routine tooth extraction.

Dr. Reece gave us an overview of the current innovative treatments to address potential bone fractures in the spine caused by multiple myeloma. Kyphoplasty is used to treat painful compression fractures in the spine. In a compression fracture, all or part of a spine bone collapses. The procedure is also called balloon kyphoplasty. A needle is placed through the skin and into the spine bone. Real-time x-ray images are used to guide the doctor to the correct area in your lower back. A balloon is placed through the needle, into the bone, and then inflated. This restores the height of the vertebrae. Cement is then injected into the space to make sure it does not collapse again.

## The Dental Clinic

The doctors made an urgent referral to the Princess Margaret Dental Clinic. Mina was scheduled to start on bisphosphonate therapy pending the opinion of the dentistry team and need for any interventions. The hospital dental clinic would evaluate her dental health and extract any problem teeth prior to getting the bisphosphonate therapy.

On May 1, 2019, we returned to the hospital for an appointment with the dental clinic. Mina was experiencing much more significant pain in her hips and her spine. The previous bone marrow biopsy was really causing some distress. She had to take pain-killing medication at least three times that day. We were anxious to get the dental clearance resolved so that we could move on to the bone strengthening therapy.

Dr. Venditelli performed a dental examination to evaluate any risk factors that could result in complications from the planned zoledronic acid (Zometa) therapy. He indicated that Mina needed to have two upper teeth extracted and one cavity fixed prior to the start of the bone strengthening therapy. Later, the clinic note stated that five teeth were to be removed. Fortunately, this turned out to be a typo, much to our relief!

# Tita Mila : Our Family Friend and Caregiver

In 1982, Mina and Mila met in Singapore, during their stint as overseas foreign workers and became steadfast friends, remaining closely connected with each other right up to the present day. Mina cannot express how important their friendship is. They went through thick and thin together for four years in Singapore, finally realizing an opportunity to immigrate to Canada.

They both found a better life in Canada, working together in the Cayne's Super Housewares Store for over thirty years. When health problems struck Mina, she did not think she could stay strong through all this time without Mila's endless support and very special unconditional love. Tita Mila was just like a sister to Mina. Without her, recuperation from Mina's health challenges would have been extremely difficult.

Mila always understood Mina, regardless of the circumstances, whether Mina was in good or poor health. It feels so amazing when someone understands, cares for you and is a loyal friend, always ready to commit one hundred percent to you. Mila could be sometimes challenging to deal with and often misunderstood, but her opinions were always welcome and often offering an invaluable contribution as a friend and a caregiver.

During Mina's multiple myeloma journey, Mila tirelessly would arrive at the hospital after a hard day's work to bring food, clothing and necessities, without a single complaint. After Mina's hospital stay, Mila's undying support continued at home. Having a dedicated family caregiver like Mila is a priceless addition, both in terms of emotional, physical and social support. We are truly blessed and owe her a huge debt of gratitude. We will be forever thankful!

# A Visitor from Italy

On May 3, 2019, Mina's sister Cita arrived from Italy. We headed to the airport to pick her up at 8 p.m. We were looking forward to having additional family support, if only for three weeks. The Canadian Embassy in Manila had repeatedly denied a compassionate request for a tourist visa to have Mina's niece visit and provide caregiver support. Apparently, the Canadian government is quite happy to take people's visa application money and then simply deny the request.

This was quite outrageous given that the government had just approved the entry into Canada of 50,000 political refugees. Needless to say, we were not impressed with the inaction and political opportunism displayed by our duly elected representatives. Don't get me wrong. I am all in favour of providing assistance to refugees. But there must be some limits to this humanitarian effort. Charity begins at home.

The next day, our group of running friends, called the 'Fast Friends' dropped by to celebrate with us and to lend their moral support. It was also a birthday celebration for our daughter Sophia. The Fast Friends expressed their desire to do some gardening for us, but in the end, we persuaded them to just come over and relax with spirited conversation while enjoying wine and food. They did bring over a fuchsia plant that we promptly installed in the front garden. The afternoon was filled with friendly banter as we all gathered around the living room to consume fine wine and food.

Liz and George are a couple who both had worked within the Canadian correctional system. They were both long-time YMCA members who ran with us regularly on Wednesday evenings and Saturday mornings. George kept everyone entertained, relating his experiences in Canada's far north as a clinical psychologist who had contracts with the government to conduct clinical evaluations for criminals as part of the court ordered assessments. George was a former probation officer with the federal government and had recently obtained his doctorate.

He also gave us some extremely funny accounts of his annual physical check-ups with his family doctor. During the prostate exam, he noticed grease bumps along the wall, next to the examination table. As his doctor performed the digital inspection, George's body jolted forward and he left his own grease bump on the wall, solving the mystery.

Alan and Kemela are another wonderful couple who also supported us during our cancer crisis. Alan has an established dental practice in the community, where Kemela also worked. Both had a taste of early retirement when the COVID-19 lockdowns were implemented. Sadly, the pandemic prevented our group from an in-person attendance at their wedding in August, 2020.

Alan was the only one of our group who also successfully completed not only the Boston Marathon but also a full Ironman Triathlon in Lake Placid, New York. Alan also trained very hard on a stationary bike in his basement to enable completion of a cross-Canada odyssey with a team of cyclists. We were all there on the sidelines cheering him on as he passed by our neighbourhood in Toronto. Although my annual running mileage usually is the equivalent of the distance across Canada, I could not imagine completing such a feat one-shot, even on a bike. Swimming is also a skill that is completely outside my wheelhouse. I have absolutely zero bouncy and sink like a rock in water. A 2.4-mile triathlon swim followed by a 112-mile bicycle ride and then completion of a 42.2-kilometre marathon is definitely not in my future.

Lynne and Jimi are another amazing couple. I would often run into Jimi (not literally) on the indoor YMCA running track on Saturday mornings. Jimi just recently had some heart issues related to blocked arteries and fortunately was able to get timely treatment to get him back on the road to full recovery. Lynne was a competitive runner before having surgery on both knees, with a transition to speed-walking afterwards. I would often stand back in awe as she completed many race events, placing her at the top of her class in race-walking. Most of her half-marathon race performances were faster than many competitors who had run in the same events!

Fran and Peter are our long-time running friends going back to when I first started my running career almost thirty years ago. They were both long-time YMCA members before changing over to the newly-built Pan Am Centre. During our younger days, I regularly ran with Peter with the YMCA Fast Friends group. I witnessed his transformation as a runner from the ten-kilometre event culminating a few years later in the running of the Toronto Marathon. It takes a combination of intense training and determination to successfully cross the finish line of the marathon. We were all disappointed when the planned Fast Friends celebration of Fran and Peter's fiftieth wedding anniversary had to be put on hold due to the pandemic.

Melanie and Mike, another wonderful couple, often would drop by our home for coffee on Sunday afternoons before they made their way to their second home in Orillia. Melanie would treat us with a serving of her delicious home-made scones. Mina supplied her fabulous Filipino noodle dish that Melanie was eager to replicate. I felt absolutely no guilt from consuming all of those calories since my weekly running mileage would quickly burn off the calories associated with the guilty pleasures.

Janet and David, while not part of our regular running group, would usually join us in our regular Fast Friends annual celebration dinners at the historic Stone Cottage Pub. David would organize in-home performances from locally renowned musicians. Mina and I are planning on attending one of David's future events, once we all get the pandemic behind us.

For multiple myeloma patients and caregivers, the importance of having a supportive social network of friends and family is critical. They play a greater role than simply providing a simple diversion from reality. People are complex social creatures who thrive on interactions with each other. Included in this dynamic is an exchange of information and ideas. Psychological studies have looked at group versus individual decision-making. The results show that group participation provides for superior outcomes as opposed to individual efforts. You may be surprised how bouncing ideas off other people can result in paving the way to solving even the most mundane of problems.

## Mina, The Rock Star

The following Tuesday, Mina, Cita and I headed to the Princess Margaret Hospital for the second CYBOR-D chemotherapy treatment followed by a consultation with our nurse practitioner Suzanne Rowland. The blood test results from the first treatment from week ago were encouraging. Suzanne stated, "There has been a huge reduction in the lactate dehydrogenase numbers from 556 to 222. Mina, you are a rock-star."

Suzanne also indicated that the monoclonal protein and free light chain tests will continue on a monthly basis to monitor the impact of the chemotherapy induction therapy. We returned home that day with a greater sense of optimism and hope that we could beat this cancer into a prolonged remission. The fact that Mina achieved a VPGR (Very Good Partial Response) from just the initial therapy was indeed a positive sign.

# Wills and Powers of Attorney

花無百日紅： No flower can bloom for a hundred days – Chinese idiom

During the month of May, we engaged a lawyer to assist with the drafting of wills for both of us, as well as power of attorney documents for both health and financial matters. Mina and I had existing wills that were seriously out of date and in desperate need of renewal. It is somewhat depressing to contemplate one's own earthly demise, but a necessary evil.

Engaging a lawyer to produce a will is not necessarily required. There are downloadable forms from the internet that one can use to produce a do-it-yourself will which is completely legal, assuming proper witnesses sign the document. However, a lawyer can spot nuances within your own personal situation that could be important. For example, our lawyer asked me, "Do you own any firearms?" I responded, "As a matter of fact, I have a 12-guage shotgun that has been sitting in storage for the past forty years."

After learning this, the lawyer explained that it presented a serious liability, mainly for the executor who would be in charge of disposing of the assets after my death. Fortunately, the City of Toronto just happened to announce a firearms buyback program as I was finalizing the will. I was able to get rid of the firearm and receive a $200 gift card in return. Problem solved!

No matter what your personal situation is, a cancer diagnosis or not, it is simply good estate planning to ensure the disposition of your assets are handled in accordance with one's wishes. Otherwise, dying without a proper will can be problematic. The government could step in and make the disposition decisions based on their rules.

The power of attorney is also a critical legal document, especially concerning healthcare. If you or your loved one becomes incapable of making health-related decisions, the power of attorney provides a legal avenue for someone that you have designated to make the choices on your behalf. For example, you can direct that no heroic life-sustaining efforts should be made in the event that you are lying comatose in a hospital bed.

The financial power of attorney is also a key legal document. If your loved one becomes incapacitated, you will need legal authority in order to conduct financial transactions on their behalf. Mortgages, loans, income tax, utility and credit cards still need to be paid. The power of attorney will allow the legal right to conduct transactions with the respective financial institutions.

Keep in mind that the power of attorney is only valid while your loved one is still alive. In the unfortunate event of either you or your loved one's passing, the Will is the only valid legal document which must be submitted, along with other documents, through the court system, known as probate. This process can be relatively time-consuming for the person named as executor in the Will. If you are not comfortable filling out legal documents, feel free to consult a lawyer or a paralegal for assistance. Whether or not you get the assistance of a lawyer, the entire process takes about eighteen months to complete.

# A Visit to the Emergency Room

Mother's Day was on May 12, 2019. Although Mina never had the opportunity to experience the joy of raising a child, she was the world's best mom to my daughter Sophia. To celebrate the day, I drove Mina, her sister Cita and her best friend Mila to Niagara Falls. It was a very rainy, breezy and cold spring day, certainly not ideal for touristy activities. Despite the weather, we made the most of our time, taking photos in front of the falls and then finishing with lunch at The Cork, one of the local restaurants in Niagara-on-the-Lake. We ended the day with dinner at Mina's cousin's home in Toronto.

Visiting the Niagara region is always special to me as it brings back memories of one of my favourite race events, the Niagara Ultra. A few years back, I ran one of my best 100-km races, starting at Niagara-on-the-Lake, running along the bike path into Niagara Falls, and then turning around right at the Falls. Of course, when the runners get back to the start/finish line, they have to do the loop again, in order to run the 100-km distance. It is an extremely challenging event to complete since the race is held in the middle of summer with a blazing sun beating down on you.

A few days later, on May 16th, Dr. Monteiro at the Mount Sinai Hospital had scheduled Mina for a core biopsy of a lymph node in her neck. The node was slightly enlarged and so he needed to sample it for any cancer cells. He had earlier attempted to get a sample from the lymph node by using a fine needle aspiration, but was not successful. He referred us to the Toronto General Hospital where they had specialists who could perform a core biopsy using ultrasound to guide a much larger instrument to get a suitable sample.

While we were in the waiting room, I noticed a fellow who had accompanied a family member to a core biopsy procedure. He seemed to be in some emotional distress as he was talking with the attending physician. "What do you mean that she passed away? How can that be possible? It was just supposed to be a standard core biopsy!"

Upon hearing this conversation, it set off a sense of panic and dread within myself. I thought to myself, "Oh my God. What have we gotten ourselves into?" As we took Mina into the procedure room, I had to keep reassuring myself that this was strictly a routine procedure and that the doctors were all experts in this field.

After the doctor explained to me how the procedure would be performed, I reluctantly had to wait outside the room in the hallway. It was only a twenty-minute operation but the time seemed to drag on forever. When they finally called me back inside, I could tell right away that Mina was in significant distress. She was in tears and complaining about feeling a possible heart attack in the making. She was having extreme pain in her chest and her back when breathing.

The doctors immediately wheeled her into another room to take x-ray images. To our relief, the x-rays came back negative for any issues. Regardless of the results, I insisted that she be taken downstairs to the emergency room to be evaluated. The doctors who did the biopsy did not think it was necessary but they did accommodate our request.

The emergency room is definitely not my favourite place. We arrived at 1:45 p.m. and were not placed into a clinic room until 3:55 p.m. After the doctors took some initial vitals, it was a very long wait until Mina was wheeled into a room next door at 8:00 p.m. to get a CT scan. While we were waiting for the scan results, I headed downstairs to get Mina some dinner. Just after I returned with the food, we received the scan results. Thankfully, there were no issues detected.

A few hours later, the emergency room doctor arrived to discuss the results with us. With no issues found on either the x-rays or the CT scan, she indicated that the core biopsy procedure sometimes causes major irritation to the nerves in the chest area. We were discharged from the emergency room at 11:30 p.m. and returned home exhausted after a very long and stressful day.

Cita had not accompanied us to the hospital since it was supposed to be a routine procedure. This event taught us all a lesson that nothing is routine or can be taken for granted when it comes to hospital visits. We received the results of the core biopsy on May 27th, 2019. Thankfully, the results were negative for metastatic cancer.

## Avoiding Infections in Pre-COVID Times

Multiple myeloma patients have compromised immune systems. All of the good foot soldiers in the bone marrow get crowded out by the evil plasma cells. This provides a golden opportunity for a nasty viral or bacterial infection to unleash its fury on the body. That is why the health guidelines necessitated by COVID-19 such as mask wearing, social distancing, avoiding crowds and regular hand washing have been practiced by myeloma folks long before the coronavirus was a gleam in any scientist's eyes.

A few days after the core biopsy debacle, Mina was well enough to go out to the mall with Cita and a group of our friends from Montreal. When we got to the shopping mall, I noticed that she forgot to bring along a face mask, which she normally wore if we were going to be around throngs of people. I hurried over to the nearest pharmacy and purchased a box of the disposable surgical masks. I insisted that she wear it and only remove it when we went for dinner at one of the restaurants in the mall. In retrospect, I came to regret that we ever went to the shopping mall that day.

The next day, I recorded Mina's medications, vitals and symptoms in the daily journal. She had the usual rib pain, fatigue, and weakness associated with myeloma. However, she reported two new symptoms, a headache and a cough. Her body temperature and blood pressure were in the normal range. But the very next day, the cough worsened and she was coughing up phlegm. I finally said to Mina, "Perhaps going to a crowded mall for shopping and dinner was not a very good idea."

Fortunately, we had a clinic appointment to complete the first cycle of CYBOR-D induction chemotherapy. We saw a huge reduction in the Bence-Jones light chain protein, all the way down to 1,152 grams per litre, which indicated progress was being made in the fight against the disease. Mina's vitals continued to be normal.

I reported the progressively worsening cough to our nurse practitioner Suzanne, who promptly prescribed an antibiotic, azithromycin, to be taken for five days to get rid of the viral infection. However, the medicine did not seem to be working. Two days later, I noted that Mina's body temperature had spiked to 38.3 degrees, a sure sign of a fever. The productive cough continued unabated. I placed an urgent phone call to Suzanne, who became quite concerned with the fever symptoms.

She prescribed a stronger antibiotic, moxifloxacin, and then advised us to check-in at a hospital emergency clinic if the fever had not resolved by noon the next day. To our relief, the fever and cough finally resolved itself over the next few days. However, the next cycle of chemotherapy had to be deferred due to the recent infection and a reduction in Mina's kidney function.

Instead, Mina was given one hour of intravenous hydration in the chemotherapy centre. Suzanne also ordered a chest x-ray to confirm that there were no residual effects of the infection such as pneumonia. Later that evening, we gave Cita a fond farewell at the airport as she boarded a flight to return to Italy.

That day was also a momentous occasion for myself since I had now reached my full workplace pension requirements and could retire at my leisure. I was finally freed of the 'golden handcuffs' that had shackled me for the past twenty-eight years! To mark this historic event, we celebrated with a bottle of champagne, with Mina capturing me on video, doing a drunken dance.

# A Great Career Interrupted

On August 6, 2019, Mina was scheduled for her regular session of the CYBOR-D induction treatment at the Princess Margaret Hospital. She had the usual blood work done early in the morning. Then it was a bit of a wait for the afternoon chemotherapy consisting of the usual Velcade injection into her stomach, followed by the consumption of seven cyclophosphamide tablets. Later that afternoon, we were on our way back home, relieved that the chemo induction cycle was close to coming to an end after more than four months. The results of the recent twenty-four-hour urine test showed another huge reduction in the Bence-Jones protein. The stem cell transplant was just over the horizon. Any glimmer of positive news was welcomed and celebrated.

As we were driving home, Mina's manager from Cayne's Super Housewares Store called. The management had just concluded a group meeting with all of the employees and the news was not good. Intense competition from the giant online retailers had basically scuttled the small retail store businesses. Cayne's did have an online retail presence but it was not enough to stave off the threat. After thirty-two wonderful years, as the newspaper ad proclaimed, the store would be closing its doors permanently by February, 2020.

The employees would be given severance packages to soften the blow of unemployment. Mina's long-term disability payments had already ended after just six months of taking leave from her position for the oral cancer surgery in September of 2018. After all of the positive results from the myeloma chemotherapy, this was a big morale-buster. Thank-you Jeff Bezos! Thank-you Amazon!

Mina had given her heart and soul to the company right from day one. She endured long hours, abusive customers and negotiated the inevitable toxicity of office politics that plague most workplaces. In retrospect, Mina's forced retirement was probably a blessing in disguise. Although she really wanted to return to her full-time career, realistically, the upcoming stem cell transplants and on-going drug cocktails afterwards did not make that option truly feasible. We were just thankful that Jerry, the store's owner, was being generous in providing a financial cushion.

The next month, Mina would begin receiving her Canada Pension Plan and Old Age Security payments which could not have been anymore timely. Over the next few months, right up until the store shut it doors, we managed to visit with her former co-workers, watching in sadness, as they slowly disassembled the shelves as the inventory was gradually sold off. A long career had suddenly come to an end. It also got me into pondering my own retirement plans.

# Planning for the Stem Cell Transplant

In the month of June 2019, we witnessed the Toronto Raptors win their first NBA Championship title. I headed out the door at Toronto City Hall for my daily lunch-time 8-km run and was forced to immediately turn back. There were wall-to-wall people lining the streets and sidewalks which made it impossible to run anywhere downtown. The victory parade was proceeding at a glacial pace. Basketball fever in the city was never so intense.

One week later, during our third cycle of chemo treatment, we met our stem cell transplant coordinator, Julie Min, at the Princess Margaret Hospital. Since Mina was diagnosed as a high-risk myeloma patient, Dr. Reece had scheduled her for a tandem stem cell transplant. This meant that she would have two back-to-back stem cell transplants, with the second transplant completed about three months after the first one. I had previously read some of the medical research reports concerning high-risk myeloma. The conclusions all suggested that a double stem cell transplant, followed by maintenance therapy, significantly extended the remission period.

Julie explained that we could opt for either an in-patient or outpatient stem cell transplant. The in-patient procedure would require a three-week stay in the hospital while the out-patient process required that the patient stays within a fifteen-minute drive to the hospital, just in case complications arise. Regardless of the option selected, daily visits to the hospital would be required for follow-up testing and monitoring. Due to Mina's high-risk status, we chose the in-patient stay at the hospital. We were also fully covered by medical insurance for the hospital room.

I would also be required to be Mina's 24/7 caregiver for a minimum five-week period. This would be for the purpose of daily monitoring of her vitals and medications, which was what

I was already doing. I would have to negotiate with my employer for flexibility in my work hours. The plan was for me to stay with Mina in the hospital room and then walk to work, which was only a few blocks from the hospital. Fortunately, my workplace had an employee fitness centre where I could shower and change.

Mina would have an autologous stem cell transplant, meaning that her own stem cells would be mobilized, collected and then re-infused into her body after having high-dose chemotherapy to wipe out everything in her bone marrow. The term 'transplant' is really not accurate. The procedure is intended to rescue one's bone marrow, after chemotherapy, through the use of one's own stem cells, which would be collected and frozen before the chemo treatment.

The mobilization of the stem cells was scheduled for August 24th. I asked Julie what was involved with the mobilization process. She said that there are new and improved methods of collecting stem cells from patients. Years ago, they could only collect the cells through a time-consuming and painful process by extracting the stem cells directly from the bone marrow. Recently, scientists discovered that they could inject a drug, called Neupogen, which would coax the stem cells out of the bone marrow and into the bloodstream.

Once the stem cells are circulating in the blood, a special machine, similar to a dialysis machine, could pluck the stem cells directly from the blood. The stem cells would then be frozen and thawed out later when the patient is ready to have them re-infused. Once re-infused, they could regenerate the immune system that was wiped out by the high-dose chemotherapy drugs. They would collect enough stem cells for two transplants.

It sounded like a fairly straight-forward process, but I had some additional concerns. I pondered whether the stem cell collection would also scoop up the cancerous myeloma plasma cells. If they later re-infused the stem cells with the cancer cells, would this not be counter-productive? Julie complemented me on my thoughtful and relevant question. She indicated that there were several scientific research papers on the subject. Generally, it was determined that 'scrubbing' the stem cell collection to rid the collected blood of cancer cells had no impact on how long the cancer stayed in remission. Additionally, the cancerous plasma cells are somewhat fragile and tend to be destroyed by the freezing and thawing process. She ended by saying, "It is your genetics that determine when the cancer will return."

Finally, Julie advised us that additional testing had to be performed prior to the start of the stem cell transplant procedure. The collection of the stem cells was scheduled for August 28th. Prior to that, Mina would be seen by the hepatologist at the Toronto General Hospital liver clinic to test for prior Hepatitis B exposure. She would also need to complete a tuberculosis (TB) skin test with her family doctor. We would have to provide the results of the TB test via email. With the appointment concluded, we left the hospital with a ton of stem cell transplant educational material to study.

# Injections, Collections and Insertions

On August 24, 2019, we picked up the Neupogen injection kit at the hospital pharmacy. For just a half dozen vials, the pharmacist said that the total cost was $5,000, but thankfully, our medical insurance covered the bulk of the expense. We then headed to the autologous transplant unit on the 14$^{th}$ floor. The nurse injected the syringe at a ninety-degree angle into Mina's abdomen and then waited for ten seconds before removing the needle. After the injections, Mina had a throbbing pain that radiated to the front of her abdomen. The side effects would be temporary.

Although the initial doses would be provided by the staff at the Princess Margaret Hospital, the coordinator arranged the injections for the next three days to be administered by the local health clinic which was conveniently located just up the street from our home. These appointments were fairly routine with the exception of one appointment where the attending nurse had quite the attitude. She exclaimed with a rather demeaning tone, "Did you not read the instructions the hospital gave you? You can easily self-inject the Neupogen at your home!" Oh well, everyone is entitled to a bad day at the office.

After all of the Neupogen injections were completed, we had the stem cell collection procedure scheduled for August 28$^{th}$ at 8:00 a.m. at the Toronto General Hospital. After check-in, the attending nurse explained the entire process to us. Mina was then hooked up to an apheresis machine which began siphoning blood out of one arm, separating out the stem cells and then returning the residual blood back through the other arm.

The entire operation was finished at 3 p.m. We were worried that additional appointments would be required if the amount of stem cells collected did not meet the minimum volume of 136 million cells per litre. Fortunately, Mina was able to cough up more than enough volume required for two stem cell transplants. With the mission accomplished, we returned home after a very long day.

A few days later, we had a double birthday celebration for Mina and our son-in-law Carlo. Sophia presented Mina with a card, a photo of Sophia with Mina and inscription that read 'Best Mom Ever.' I wholeheartedly agreed with this sentiment. Although Mina could not have children of her own, she was the epitome of motherhood, having taken Sophia under her wing from day one, providing nurture, support and the perfect role model.

On September 12, 2019, we returned to the Toronto General Hospital for the insertion of a Hickman catheter line into Mina's chest. The Hickman line would allow the nurses to administer chemotherapy, re-infuse the stem cells and extract blood samples without the need to constantly poke Mina's arm with the standard syringes. It resembled a multi-coloured war medal. Mina jokingly said, "This will become my very best friend over the next few months!"

Although the Hickman line provided a major convenience, it had to be regularly maintained and cleaned, otherwise there would be a risk of contracting an infection. Julie, our stem cell transplant coordinator arranged for the weekly maintenance to be done at our local hospital clinic.

# The First Stem Cell Transplant

After getting the results of the recent blood tests, we received clearance for the stem cell transplant from the infectious disease experts. On September 17, 2019, Mina was admitted to the fifteenth-floor myeloma transplant in-patient unit. To our surprise, the administrator on duty was Mina's friend Melita who had immigrated from the Philippines many years ago, at about the same time as Mina. Seeing a familiar face certainly helped reduce some of the anxiety we were feeling.

Although we were only covered for a semi-private room, due to the risks of contracting an infection, we were assigned a private room which would become our home for the next three weeks. I was determined never to leave Mina's side. I had never been more resolute in my transformative role as a patient caregiver and advocate. This was my new mission in life! My presence in the unit also took some pressure away from the over-worked nursing staff. I could assist with giving her a shower and intermittently run to the on-site kitchen to get water refills. The staff commented that due to the additional caregiver support, Mina was a very low-maintenance patient.

There was a sturdy, yet uncomfortable fold-away cot that I would use as my bed. I brought along the Zopiclone and Ativan pills that my family doctor had prescribed to help me sleep and reduce anxiety. This turned out to be a Godsend since getting a decent night's sleep on the hard cot would have been impossible without a drug-assist.

Dr. Franke was the clinical associate who provided us with a briefing on the stem cell transplant process. Mina would first have to get bloodwork done, an ECG, a chest x-ray and provide a urine sample. I had to give a summary of the current medications Mina was taking, which seemed to be enough to fill a small drug store. To reduce the potential for negative drug interactions, some of the medications had to be put on hold.

Dr. Franke then taped a treatment calendar to the wall. It had sad and smiley faces on certain weekdays. The sad faces represented potential nasty side-effect days brought on by the high-dose chemotherapy. The happy faces started to appear on day number ten, where Mina could be in the recovery and healing mode.

There was a swab applied to the buttocks to test for infections such as MRSA (Methicillin-resistant Staphylococcus aureus) and VRE (Vancomycin-resistant Enterococci). I could not remember the names of these super-bugs let alone pronounce them. I only knew that they were difficult to treat given their resistance to anti-biotics. If Mina developed diarrhea during her stay, the medical team would also test for C-Difficile, a life-threatening bacterium, that often affects older adults confined to hospital settings. To our relief, the tests all came back negative a few days later.

For dinner, I headed down the street to the Duke of Cornwall pub where I had taken Mina to eat on the day that we were admitted to the transplant unit. It is an English-style pub with excellent vegetarian options. I enjoyed my meal at the bar, washing it down with some cheap London Red wine. There was one happy customer who arrived and had just finished work next door. He was friendly enough but I could tell that he had heavily pre-loaded with sauce before he even sat down. I suppose his work doing information technology was stressful and he was looking to blow off some steam. The fellow was likely a regular patron.

On the other side of me sat two Air Canada pilots. I casually asked what type of aircraft they piloted and they replied "The smallest jet in the fleet. And it is not as difficult as most people imagine." I really envy people who find their niche in life and end up doing a job that they love. Most folks really develop a dislike of their workplace, including yours truly. After returning to work, I was closely approaching the job burnout cliff and was ready to jump. If had not chosen the financial planning path, I would have become a commercial pilot. We all make choices in life that we later live to regret. The upside is that those bad choices are hopefully more than offset by the positive decisions we make, such as choosing healthy activities such as running.

The next day was labelled 'Minus One' on the transplant calendar. High dose chemotherapy using Melphalan was given via the Hickman line. After thirty minutes, the infusion was complete. To help offset any mouth sores that could develop from the chemo drug, Mina was then given ice chips to munch on. It reminded me of the sage advice given to injured runners about the importance of applying ice to the injured area to reduce inflammation and promote healing. The doctors also added some anti-biotic and anti-fungal medications, as if we really needed to add more pills to the prescription list!

We finally arrived at 'Day Zero' on the calendar. It was time to repatriate Mina's stem cells back to the rightful home in the bone marrow where they could be re-born, proliferate and give Mina a brand-new immune system. After confirming negative test results for the Herpes and Zoster viruses, the actual stem cell transplant was relatively non-eventful. A bag full of orange coloured plasma was infused over twenty minutes. Afterwards, there was the distinct sickly-sweet smell of cream corn in the room. Apparently, the smell comes from the preservative that they add when the cells are frozen. When the stem cells are thawed, the odour is released.

I was surprised that the stem cells could be re-introduced just one day after ingesting the poisonous chemotherapy. Apparently, the chemo drug clears out of the body within twenty-four hours. With the transplant finished, we just had to wait for the expected side-effects, including nausea, blurred vision, a shaky body, nerve pain and major hair loss to appear. Then it would be a matter of riding out the storm for the next two weeks.

When the ninth day arrived, Mina was feeling much better. She seemed to be recovering exactly according to the schedule outlined on Dr. Franke's calendar. However, the next day, her body temperature spiked to 37.7 degrees. The nurses said that this was almost surely the result of a bacterial infection. They gave her Piptazo via intravenous injection every eight hours along with a broad spectrum anti-biotic called Tobramycin.

Blood samples and more swabs were taken. The culture results would be available in five days. The chest x-ray came back negative for pneumonia. The swab test results were also negative for influenza. She had to be given an infusion of platelets, which are the cells that help with blood clotting.

On the tenth day, a patient in the next room to ours, passed away. He was a Filipino man who had undergone a stem cell transplant. I had previously witnessed him moving around the hallway of the unit with a walker, getting the recommended exercise as encouraged by the nursing staff. But he was in his room by himself the night that he got up from bed to go to the washroom. I suppose he did not realize how weakened and unsteady his body had become as a result of the stem cell transplant. He fell down in the washroom, hit his head and sadly succumbed to his injuries.

It was a reminder to myself as to why I had chosen to be with Mina 24/7 in the hospital. I could only imagine the heartbreak that the man's wife felt. They both had a life that was side-tracked by a diagnosis of multiple myeloma. They were given hope of a better quality of life through a treatment program. And then it all came crashing down. It was a very unfair and cruel fate indeed. It reminded of the Chinese idiom 'Man proposes but God disposes.' (謀事在人,成事在天).

When Day #12 arrived, we were informed that Mina could be discharged from the hospital the very next day. Claudia, our attending nurse, shaved Mina's head, which had steadily lost most of her locks as the result of the chemotherapy. Although on the road to recovery, Mina was still very weak with a shaky body and chills. We were given instructions to call 9-1-1 in the event that any severe symptoms developed after we returned home. It was absolutely essential to avoid infections.

This meant that Mina could not ride on public transit, or go grocery shopping or do gardening. Whenever she had follow-up hospital clinic visits, she was advised to wear a face mask. We were basically given COVID-19 safety instructions months before the disease even emerged. The next day we were discharged in the late afternoon. We headed home, grateful that the first stem cell transplant was behind us while knowing that the second transplant was just over the horizon.

# The Second Stem Cell Transplant

Mina required regular check-ups and monitoring while recovering from the first stem cell transplant. She wore one of my running buffs while waiting for her hair to re-grow. Shortly after discharge from the hospital, she developed a nagging cough, mild fever, an elevated heart-rate and shortness of breath. Often, the symptoms are related to the high dose chemotherapy.

There were regular trips back to the hospital clinic. Most patients require an average of three visits post stem cell transplant. Suzanne Rowland prescribed codeine to treat the dry, hacking cough. Further blood work and a chest x-ray were needed. The doctors discovered an infection in her left chest. She took a prescription cough syrup, more anti-biotics and had to reduce her fluid intake. They canceled the upcoming minor surgery to fix the scar tissue on her neck, a souvenir from the oral cancer surgery. We prayed for a full recovery before the second transplant, scheduled for December. Mina's friend Myrna stayed with her during the day, while I was crunching the financial numbers at work.

On October 21, 2019, I voted in Canada's federal election, but my head was in such a fuzzy state, I don't even remember who I had voted for or even which political party. All I remember is that one politician was re-elected with a minority government, despite a blackface scandal when he was a drama teacher. The funneling of two-hundred and fifty-thousand dollars to his family through a charity also did not hurt his cause. Wining and dining wealthy Chinese tycoons in a 'pay-to-play' scheme, rationalized as a means to help the middle-class, was another head-scratcher. Or perhaps I voted for the guy who used his party's political fund to finance his kid's education at an elite private school.

This type of comedy writes itself in Canadian politics, similar to the right-wing Trumpian political madness south of our border. Unfortunately, there is no high-dose chemo treatment available for the political cancer that spreads through either voter malaise, willful ignorance or by conspiracy theories. It seems that the very act of exercising our democratic voting right results in an instantaneous relapse of regret or a severe case of voter's remorse.

## MMRF Toronto Patient Summit

On November 9, 2019, the Multiple Myeloma Research Foundation (MMRF) held its very first Canadian Patient Summit in Toronto. We pre-registered for the event which was held at the Sheraton Centre Hotel, right across from my workplace at Toronto City Hall. Dr. Reece, who is Mina's hematologist, would be one of the keynote speakers and presenters. We were thankful that the big pharmaceutical companies provided financial support to allow this event to happen. The organizers provided a complimentary breakfast and lunch along with helpful information brochures on multiple myeloma.

All attendees were provided with a tablet that could display the presentation slides. We could also send questions directly to the presenters, who would respond during the Q&A session. As various topics were presented, my brain lit up with a ton of myeloma questions. I could barely keep up, simultaneously listening to the speakers while typing in my queries.

Before the conference, I had viewed several information videos on the Multiple Myeloma Research Foundation's website. There was one notable video in which the implications of the innovative CRISPR technology were outlined. The acronym CRISPR refers to 'Clustered Regularly Interspaced Short Palindromic Repeats', one heck of a tongue-twister. It is basically a technology that can be used to edit genes. The application of this new science to multiple myeloma eluded me.

I posed the following question to the doctors, "What are the implications of CRISPR in the future treatment of multiple myeloma?" Their first reaction to the question was, "Wow, we see there is a certain level of sophistication in the audience today!" They went on to explain CRISPR in quite a technical fashion, which probably went over everyone's heads, including my own. Generally, I got the sense that the technology could be applied to making myeloma CAR-T cell therapy more durable, since the re-engineered T-Cells tend to get exhausted in less than one year. In any event, it was encouraging to see the potential for this novel technology to one day be integral in a cure for the disease. Wouldn't it be really great if the scientists could modify the CAR-T cells by adding this gene-editing tool to enable direct repair to the cellular machinery?

The conference also had break-out sessions where the participants could choose to attend a smaller group discussion on specific topics hosted by two doctors for each session. We chose the group that was hosted by Dr. Reece. There were some slides that reviewed the basics of multiple myeloma as well as a summary of the tools that the medical team uses in the diagnosis and monitoring of the disease.

One chart that caught my attention was the graph which showed the M-spike protein, a key indicator of myeloma. I was interested in learning about the specific components of the M-spike and whether it reflected the free light chains as well as the monoclonal protein. The previous day, I had received Mina's IgD monoclonal protein and free light chain results, which showed a huge improvement. As such, my query into this particular presentation slide was of great relevance to me. The first stem cell transplant appeared to have knocked back the myeloma into a good remission.

I don't believe that my question was as clear as I could have expressed it and so the answer that I received was somewhat vague. I later did some online research where I viewed a video entitled, 'Know your labs.' It provided me with a very clear and concise summary of the M-spike chart and the components. Apparently, the light chains are so 'light', that they move right through the electrically charged gel and would not be reflected in the M-spike. This is why separate serum blood and urine testing is critical to understanding the light chain proteins.

# Welcome to Retirement

A few days later, I handed in my retirement notice to my manager. Although my family doctor had given me the go-ahead to return to work the previous March, it was obvious that I could not focus on my job and be an effective myeloma caregiver at the same time. The workplace had a toxic atmosphere during my 28-year tenure and recent organizational changes resulted in further deterioration of the office environment.

It got to the point where I absolutely hated getting up at 5 a.m., enduring a crowded subway commute to work, capped off with a tortuous seven hours crunching the budget for the City of Toronto. As soon as I returned home from work, I popped an anti-anxiety drug called Ativan, which assisted with an instant reduction in my stress level. There was simply not enough liquor in my cabinet to deal with it. If only I could press the rewind button on my life and choose a more rewarding career path, perhaps becoming a renowned Anthropologist or failing that, a rocket scientist!

I had handed in my retirement letter on the day the budget was launched. I had just completed my toughest career marathon in history, crossing the finish line, leaving a legacy of accomplishments and near-successes! I began my journey, crossing the race start line at Carleton University, graduating in 1979 with a B. Comm. (Honours) with a specialization in high Finance and Economics. This was the same university that one of our former illustrious Mayors attended. Although I had also participated in the same rowdy fraternity parties, the result was a successful outcome and I actually graduated. No one was more surprised than yours truly.

My educational highlights included a ground-breaking research paper that resulted in top marks in a Business Policy Seminar course. The research paper was entitled 'Subliminal Advertising as a Marketing Strategy: Fact or Fiction?' This was a critical analysis which integrated a complex psychological theory with current marketing strategies. The paper argued against the dynamics of subliminal advertising, basically concluding that the whole premise of the approach was false.

Unbeknownst to my professor, I had embedded subliminal and Freudian messages within the body of his research paper, with such phrases as 'This research paper is worthy of an A+ grade'. The Professor commented that the paper was an exceptionally stimulating read. To which I replied, "I bet it was Sir!"

After graduation, I purchased some loud plaid suits and went to work as a computer salesman with NCR Canada, going door-to-door in Ottawa, pushing obsolete computers that were enormous in size and slow, compared with the today's state-of-the-art systems. These goliath machines barely fit in the back of my 1977 Chevy Nova. Many times, I would be quickly shown the door by company Presidents who uttered similar phrases such as, "It's a nice day outside, and so you should take a walk." After enduring one year of this 'real-world experience', I was now very well prepared for my next adventure...a career in Budgeting and Financial Planning!

I relocated to the Northwest Territories, and began a career as a Budget Analyst working tirelessly under the Midnight Sun, crafting budgets for several departmental programs. Nights were spent at the infamous Gold Range Hotel, with drunken karaoke singing and dreams of living in a warmer climate. Global warming? Global swarming! The weather was not warm in my local area! I made the most of my northern adventure, learning some of the indigenous language and culture, and sampling raw whale blubber, ultimately leading to my decision to turn vegetarian.

I then relocated to Montreal to start a new career as a Product Specialist with Future Electronics, working very long hours, buying and selling, selling and buying high technology semiconductor products. I transformed my product line from $100,000 per month in sales to over $1 million per month! I became the 'Donald Trump' of the semiconductor business world, but without most of the corruption.

The company offered me a Product Manager position in London, England, but I eventually turned it down in order to take a position as a Marketing Representative, dealing in gas fireplaces and humidifiers. Despite my semi-best efforts, the company went into Chapter Eleven bankruptcy. I then moved on to my next career, rising from the ashes and being re-born as a Budget Analyst with Superior Propane. Eventually, I ran out of gas and moved on to become a Budget Officer with the former City of Scarborough in 1991, prior to the City merging with the City of Toronto.

My introduction to municipal budgeting was, at first, a rude awakening. Why were citizens angry that their property taxes were rising by mere triple digits every year? This was among some of the questions I had attempted to address when delivering the Works & Environment Department's budget to the Scarborough City Council. The City Councillors were a well-intentioned albeit misguided group who enjoyed scoring political points at the expense of the 'budget messenger.' They asked intelligent, thoughtful questions such as "Hcy, thc ncw Budget Officer is losing his hair." To which I quickly replied, "Yep, but it is genetic." At the end of the day, I was given an award by the City Manager for 'most innovative budget presentation.'

During my career, I had enrolled in the Psychology Specialist Program at the University of Toronto, Scarborough campus, excelling at designing social psychology experiments, that almost adhered to ethical standards. I conducted a ground-breaking research project which compared community-based policing in poor neighborhoods with affluent neighborhoods in Toronto. The results of the pseudo-scientific study were quite telling. Many of the self-medicated residents of the poorer areas of the City possessed greater intellect and cognitive abilities than their well-healed cousins. This study may have resulted in social change and the re-thinking of approaches to community-based policing and carding, but I could not provide definitive empirical support to back up this claim.

And then, in 1998, we experienced the Mike Harris 'Common Sense Revolution' which was political code language designed to attack the evils of socialism. Imagine handing out public money to support the down-trodden in society? Whatever happened to the principle of individual responsibility? The local municipalities were socialist enclaves that had become a cancer on society. And with a stroke of the pen, the amalgamation of the City of Toronto became a done deal, despite howls of protest from the local fiefdoms. I then headed downtown to Metro Hall to work with colleagues from the former municipalities, cobbling together the first amalgamated City budget, which is still experiencing 'growing pains' to this very day.

Later on, I joined the City's Mentorship Program, successfully assisting many new immigrants with career search and placement. As part of a cross-cultural initiative, I self- studied Mandarin and learned many useful idiomatic Chinese phrases such as 'Thirteen o'clock', 'Your wife put a green hat on your head', 'Straddle two boats' and 'The greedy snake tries to swallow the whole elephant.' I enjoyed real-life language practice with many of my Mandarin-speaking colleagues, increasing my language fluency so that my pronunciation now became pretty darn close to being understandable. There you have it, Paul Chenery, 'a master of all trades and a Jack of none', or something like that. Mission Accomplished!

Upon learning of my planned retirement, one of my running friends said to me, "It is called burnout my friend. You certainly don't need more aggravation and stress loaded on top of your plate at this stage." I wholeheartedly agreed with this assessment and happily handed in my retirement notice, with my final day at work scheduled for January 10, 2020. The remaining two months at work seemed to drag on forever. However, my final week coincided with the conclusion of Mina's second stem cell transplant, which turned out to be very timely, given that all hell was about to break loose a few months later with the COVID-19 pandemic.

## Stem Cell Transplant Number Two

Prior to Mina's second stem cell transplant, scheduled for mid-December 2019, she underwent several follow up visits with the nephrologist and the hematologists. Dr. Kitchlu, the nephrologist, indicated that Mina's kidney function had improved, giving the all-clear for the next stem cell transplant. Dr. Reece had recommended a lower dose that would normally be given for the melphalan chemo drug during the first transplant, which likely reduced the negative impact on her kidneys. The results from the December 12th blood tests were also positive, indicating normal free light chain proteins and immune system function.

Finally, the hospital's dentist gave us the go-ahead but strongly advised Mina not to have major dental surgery or tooth extractions performed by the family dentist. After the transplant, a new bone-strengthening monoclonal antibody drug, Denosumab, could be considered to replace the monthly Zometa infusions. Apparently, Denosumab is much easier on kidney function.

On December 19, 2019, Mina was again admitted to the Princess Margaret Hospital stem cell transplant ward, with her long-time friend Melita greeting us. It was like déjà vu all over again. Blood and urine samples were taken, along with the standard MRSA and VRE bacterial swab testing. The cytomegalovirus test showed a low positive result, which was somewhat concerning. The ECG, chest x-ray and urinalysis were all normal.

The following day, Mina was given the high-dose chemo to wipe out everything in her bone marrow (again). Prior to that, there were several pre-med dosing of anti-nausea drugs, and dexamethasone via intravenous infusion along with a supply of ice chips to munch on.

In the evening, I took a sleeping pill and settled down on the rock-hard cot, arising the next morning to run five kilometres on the indoor YMCA track, just a fifteen-minute walk from the hospital. I continued with my medium distance training run with my friend Olex, running 23 kilometres the next day along the Toronto waterfront, in freezing rain and blowing wind. I was totally soaked and chilled to the bone. After that, I felt proud to have endured another tough weather day running outside, but thankful to get back to the warmer confines of the hospital room with Mina.

The second transplant proceeded much the same way as the previous one. The second bag of stem cells was thawed, quickly infused and the smell of cream corn was again overwhelming. Mina experienced fairly minor side effects, including fatigue, shaky knees and stomach cramps. All blood lab results and kidney function tests reflected normal levels.

During our extended hospital stay, we were very thankful to our network of family and friends who dropped in constantly to support us. Mina's friend Mila, visited every day, providing take-out food and laundry service. I was extremely grateful since I required fresh running outfits after working up a sweat on my regular lunch-time and evening training runs.

On Christmas day, our daughter Sophia and son-in-law Carlo paid us a visit. They gave me a few of my favourite IPA beers and a new Amazon fire computer tablet. I saved the beer for when we returned home. The computer tablet was really a bonus since we could now binge on Netflix movies to pass time during Mina's extended recovery. I must have consumed a boatload of horror films, my favourite genre, although these films did not exactly do anything for my stress levels.

For the next few days, I had to wear full personal protective gear. Mina had experienced some diarrhea and so additional tests for the C-difficile bacterium were conducted. As a precaution, I was given a full yellow gown, blue gloves, a face shield and medical mask. This equipment had to be removed and discarded every time I exited the hospital room, if only to get Mina some water. This was extremely cumbersome but not as difficult as trying to get a good night's sleep wearing all of that stuff. Even the sleeping pills did little to help me overcome the level of discomfort! The C-difficile tests came back negative and I was relieved to get rid of the extra protective gear that had me in a cocoon-like grip.

On December 27th, my sixty-third birthday had arrived. I had never expected to celebrate it in a hospital ward. Mina sent me the following email birthday greeting:

"To my super-awesome, wonderful husband. I am so grateful I married someone like you. You have brought so much hope, joy and happiness into my life especially when I needed it the most. You are one of a kind. No one else can surpass your patience, compassion, thoughtfulness, encouragement and support to me. With each passing day, I become stronger and better all because of you being here, always on my side. I am so blessed and forever grateful so today my dearly beloved husband, we celebrate your special day, just the two us in this hospital room, nice and simple but every moment will be treasured because they are so special. Happy birthday my one and only honeybun. Love you forever."

The final week of the hospital stay was mostly unremarkable. For several days, Mina required supplementary magnesium via intravenous infusions. There were also anti-bacterial and anti-fungal medications that were administered daily, including ciprofloxacin and fluconazole. Regular Neupogen infusions were provided, to allow for the stimulation of neutrophils, a type of white blood cell that protects against infections.

We celebrated New Year's Day in the hospital. Our friends Peter and Fran, who are part of our running group, dropped by for a welcome visit. Peter is a survivor of stage three prostate cancer. He was a long-time member at the local YMCA who, prior to his cancer diagnosis, ran with our group on Wednesday evenings and Saturday mornings. I would often see Fran at the gym, usually participating in the morning yoga classes. While I love all forms of exercise, I tried a yoga class just once and discovered that it was too slow for my liking. No wonder my running muscles are forever tight. I am terrible when it comes to committing to a regular stretching routine.

The next day, Sharon, a spiritual advisor at the hospital, offered her support. While I was not brought up with a strong religious practice, Mina was totally devoted to her faith and would find daily prayer a soothing antidote. Sharon inquired as to how we were both coping. We responded, "We both have a strong sense of hope and optimism, as well as a certainty that the Lord will look after us. We have accepted this outcome and have committed to make the most of the fantastic support we have received from everyone." On that note, Sharon seemed satisfied that we were handling our situation appropriately.

After Sharon finished her visit, Mike and Melanie, another wonderful couple from our running group, paid us a surprise visit. Mike was my regular training partner on the Wednesday night runs. We would meet at the local YMCA after work and run 11 kilometres through the park. Mike was retired from the tax department but would often give me sound financial advice related to income tax matters and investments. Melanie, was into power-walking, which is just as effective as running in terms of burning calories. Several years ago, she walked with Mina in the Ottawa half-marathon, while I busted myself in the full marathon, finishing in 3:04.

The next day, in the early afternoon, we were discharged from the hospital. With the second transplant now behind us, the plan was to start maintenance drug therapy within three months. The goal of the maintenance program would be to extend the remission for as long as possible while maintaining a good quality of life. Typically, a three-drug regimen would be prescribed along with a bone-strengthening drug. We now just had to wait patiently for Mina to recover her strength and re-grow her hair, while constantly avoiding the risk of infection.

We returned to the Princess Margaret transplant day hospital on January 16, 2020. This was a momentous day for Mina. After receiving some intravenous hydration, she had some routine blood work performed. Finally, the Hickman line, Mina's best friend for the past six months was removed. As we exited the unit, the nurses invited Mina to ring the bell to signal the completion of her long transplant ordeal. The other patients and nursing staff applauded loudly as we celebrated this tradition. We returned home with a renewed sense of hope.

We had a follow-up appointment with the hematology clinic in late February. We met with Dr. Bautista, an intern working with Dr. Reece. Since Dr. Bautista was originally from the Philippines, this was a bonus for Mina, since they could switch back and forth between English and Tagalog as needed. Mina was in a complete remission, based on the latest test results. The upcoming maintenance drug therapy would consist of taking 5 mg of Revlimid for life. Mina would also take 2.3 mg of Ninlaro, an oral proteasome inhibitor for one year, along with dexamethasone. The provincial health plan covered the cost of Revlimid. For Ninlaro, we applied to the drug's manufacturer, Takeda Oncology for compassionate use, which was approved. Both of these medications would be unaffordable without a government or private healthcare plan.

Prior to commencing the maintenance drug therapy, Mina had another routine blood test to screen for the myeloma protein. Although the immune system and kidney function were normal, she experienced a slight relapse in the free lambda light chain protein. There was also a trivial spike in the monoclonal protein. The need to start on the maintenance drugs became an urgent priority.

A few days later, on March 28, 2020, I picked up the drug cocktail from the hospital pharmacy. We were provided with a handy calendar which outlined each day in the three-week cycle and the dosing requirements. The Revlimid would be taken every other day while both the Ninlaro and the Dexamethasone would be on the menu every Saturday. Mina had to ensure that the Ninlaro be taken on an empty stomach. Low dose aspirin also had to be administered daily, to prevent blood clots that could result from the Revlimid dosing.

Given the volume of maintenance and standard drugs that Mina had to consume, I made two separate sub-sections in the daily medical diary to keep things straight. We could not afford to screw up on the drug dosing schedule. I also made it a point to record any new symptoms that developed which could be related to the new treatment. The only significant new side effects were some blurred vision and skin rash, along with dark urine, which tended to be temporary.

Mina was tolerating the maintenance therapy with the same resilience she had demonstrated throughout this epic journey! We were approaching the one-year anniversary since Mina's myeloma diagnosis, initial therapy, stem cell transplants and the beginning of the maintenance program. The year passed with lightning speed. My first daily diary book was finished. I placed an online order for another two journals. I viewed these records as a treasure and a reminder of my duty as a determined patient caregiver and advocate.

On a sad note, we were notified on April 11th, that Mina's brother Danny had passed away. He was working as a chef in Dubai when he suddenly developed chest pains. He made it to the hospital but did not recover. They said the cause of death was heart failure, but we could not rule out the possibility that COVID-19 was a contributory factor. His employer arranged for Danny's body to be returned to the Philippines for a proper funeral. Unfortunately, the COVID-19 pandemic was in full force which meant that the lockdown thwarted Mina's family efforts to hold a regular memorial service.

# Elevated Heart Rate

During the course of Mina's maintenance cycle, I continued to diligently record the three-week cycle of drug cocktail dosing and any new symptoms. She was tolerating the therapy quite well, with only the expected fatigue, body weakness, temporary blurred vision, muscle cramps and the occasional skin rash on her face, back and legs.

Saturdays were the highlight of the drug maintenance program, which usually consisted of Dexamethasone, Ninlaro, Revlimid and low-dose Aspirin. I was thankful that our friend Mila could stay with Mina during the mornings while I was pounding the pavement on my long runs. We were always on guard for any negative drug side effects that would require immediate action.

By June 2020, we had arrived at the third month of the program. Mina began to experience a significantly heart rate with the slightest amount of exertion. At first, we reasoned that it was due to the steroid energy boost provided by the Dexamethasone. She took Ativan as a sedative, which did help settle down her pulse and was useful as a sleep aid. However, the abnormally high blood pressure and heart rate continued.

Dr. Kitchlu, our nephrologist, performed a series of blood tests to monitor the kidney function, since Mina had Type II diabetes which seemed to be adversely affecting her kidneys. Her blood sugar and A1C were at levels that indicated mild to moderate kidney disease. The creatinine would often be at abnormal levels and the kidney filtration rate was low. He advised Mina to start on a new blood pressure medication called Telmisartan which is an angiotensin receptor blocker (ARB) designed to relax the blood vessels to allow blood to flow more easily.

I did some internet research in advance of the appointment with Dr. Kitchlu. I had read that a risk factor for developing a severe case of COVID-19 is high blood pressure, since the virus attaches at the ACE receptor site, the same location that many blood pressure medications act on. Dr. Kitchlu was surprised that I had picked up on this risk and indicated that the science related to this was still not determined. He would follow-up in three months with additional tests. He also said that there was a new class of drugs called Sodium Glucose Co-Transporter2 (SGTL2) inhibitors, called gliflozins, that could be useful, along with Mina's Metformin dosing, to help with blood sugar control and provide cardiovascular benefits. Later on, we learned that she would not be eligible to use the SGTL2 inhibitor due to the cancer treatments.

As a patient advocate, I indicated to Dr. Kitchlu's associate, Dr. Skartic, that the Telmisartan blood pressure medication had resulted in abnormally low blood pressure. I also asked him, "Mina is taking a proton pump inhibitor, called Pantoprazole to offset nausea. Do you have any concerns with that drug's impact on kidney function?" Dr. Skartic paused and then asked me, "Do you work in the medical field?" I replied that I did not, but had conducted some online research on which types of drugs could adversely affect kidney function. He stated that it was fine to continue with the daily Pantoprazole dose.

He advised us to stop the Telmisartan but then suggested that we take our blood pressure machine to a pharmacy and then compare the home blood pressure readings to the machine readings in the drug store. Of course, as soon as we got to the pharmacy, we realized that the devices were out of order due to the COVID pandemic. As a backup plan, in my daily medical journal, I had started to record three daily readings of Mina's blood pressure and pulse.

On a regular basis, I loaded the data into a spreadsheet and then plugged in a formula to compute the average blood pressure over several months. I had two separate data sets, one for the period of time Mina was taking the Telmisartan and the other set to record the data without the blood pressure meds. The results confirmed that Mina's blood pressure was quite normal without the Telmisartan. I suppose that all of my years crunching budget numbers into spreadsheets finally paid off!

# Medical Records Held Hostage

In July of 2020, Mina's long-time family physician, Dr. Ling, announced that she would be retiring. We started to panic after hearing this news since Mina needed to have all of her childhood vaccinations re-done which is required after stem cell transplants. Dr. Ling promptly transferred all of Mina's medical records to a private data storage company who would take stewardship of the records until we coughed up $174 to get access to them. I initially objected to the quoted price since the letter from Dr. Ling indicated a total cost of $94. The pushy sales person at the other end of the line retorted with, "Oh, that price only covers the first 100 pages. Your file consists of quite a volume and so the $174 covers the additional pages." It sounded to me like a classic bait and switch ruse. I was really surprised that the Province of Ontario would actually support such a scheme.

Imagine your personal medical records being held hostage by a private company! Not only that, but a representative of the company continued to hound us to buy the records and issued a very stern warning, "The new family doctor will not take you as a patient until you get your medical records!"

In my opinion, this sounded like a desperate sales pitch, which required some investigation. Whenever I smell something funny, I like to put it to the smell test with my bullshit meter. I first had to negotiate some bureaucratic red tape with the health care system, deregistering Mina's provincial health card with her former family doctor and then requested the agency search for a new general practitioner for Mina.

We found a very competent family doctor conveniently located just a few blocks from our home. At the first meet and greet interview, I asked her, "Do you really need Mina's old medical files? It is a huge amount of paper and the data company wants us to pay $174." She indicated that the old file would not be very useful and that she was going forward with her own tests anyway. Upon hearing this, I planned to give that sales representative a good piece of my mind the next time she had the nerve to call us. Fortunately, the private data company had given up and we never heard from them again.

# Stress Testing

Dr. Bautista was concerned about Mina's elevated pulse and blood pressure. She advised that it would be prudent to refer us to a cardiologist for further assessment. On Thursday, June 25th, we went to the Toronto General Hospital where an echocardiogram was performed. The nurse also fitted Mina with a 72-hour heart monitor, called a Holter72. The monitor recorded Mina's cardio data over a period of three days. We returned the device on the following Sunday and awaited the results.

A few weeks later, Dr. Lee, the cardiologist at the Toronto General Hospital discussed the results of the cardiology tests. We reviewed Mina's family history, which included a terrible legacy of heart disease, specifically related to her father and many of her siblings. We both breathed a sigh of relief when the echocardiogram revealed no evidence of heart disease. This despite the data which showed Mina's average heart rate of 105 beats per minute (bpm) along with a maximum recorded value of 158 bpm. All of the cholesterol blood tests came back with normal values.

This was by no means the end of the cardiology tests. Dr. Lee referred Mina to the Toronto Western Hospital to undergo what is called a Sestamibi-Persantine stress test. This is a two-part scan. Although we were still under the COVID-19 lockdown, the staff allowed me to watch the procedure, take notes and ask questions.

In the first part of the test, Mina was injected with Sestamibi, a radioactive tracer which provides a visual image of blood flow to the heart. She had to lie under a nuclear scanner for 20 minutes with her hands held behind her head. She also had to lay perfectly still to avoid interfering with the scan. My only concern was related to the injection of the radioactive tracer and the possible negative impact on her kidneys. The technicians assured me it was safe and that the radiation dose was the equivalent of a chest x-ray.

The second scan involved a stress test. Normally, a patient would be required to walk on a treadmill and exercise as much as tolerable. The very sight of the treadmill seemed to evoke a Pavlovian response within me. I desperately wanted to hop on and get in a fast-paced run, but restrained myself. Since this was the era of COVID, heavy breathing within an enclosed room would be risky. With this in mind, they modified the test to provide for a pharmacologically induced stress. After 12 minutes, the stress scan was completed and we headed for home. The next day, Dr. Lee gave us the results. The scan showed that Mina had a normal heart function. He speculated that her elevated heart rate and blood pressure were likely due to dehydration.

Later in the afternoon, we had a telephone follow-up appointment with Dr. Bautista. The latest blood results showed Mina's free light chain lambda protein, the output of the cancerous plasma cells, had increased to 41.1 mg per litre, although the kappa to lambda ratio was still normal. To our collective relief, the IgD monoclonal protein was not detected. There could be a need to adjust the maintenance drug dosing, but the final decision would rest with Dr. Reece.

# The Endocrinologist

Of greater concern was Mina's continued elevated heart rate. Dr. Bautista suggested the level of thyroid hormone could be abnormal. We would consult with our endocrinologist, Dr. Boright, to review the current Synthroid dosing and make adjustments if needed. The recent ultrasound scan on Mina's neck was normal. There was no evidence of the thyroid cancer making a return appearance. The monitoring would continue yearly.

Due to the pandemic, our first meeting in October, 2020 with Dr. Boright was conducted virtually. Prior to the meeting, I educated myself on the function of the thyroid, including the role that the various thyroid hormones (TSH, T3, T4) play in regulating body metabolism. Any over or under production of these hormones can result in symptoms, including heart palpitations. Since Mina was relying on daily Synthroid pills to manufacture the hormones, the dosing had to be monitored and adjusted, if the lab tests revealed that they were out of balance.

With the virtual meeting underway, I asked Dr. Boright some technical questions relating to the previous blood tests which showed the thyroid hormones at abnormal levels. I noted that the thyroid stimulating hormone (TSH) was very low at .06 mIU/L, whereas the normal range should be between 0.32 to 4.0. The thyroxine (T4) was a bit too high, being measured at 21 pmol/L. He did not respond directly but instead asked me, "Are you a doctor." I replied that I was not, but instead relied primarily on Dr. Google for my knowledge. He jokingly responded, "Well, I think you are Dr. Google!"

In the end, Dr. Boright proposed a modified dose schedule for the Synthroid medication. Instead of the daily 75-mcg schedule, he recommended a dose of 50-mcg for three days of the week, with the 75-mcg tablet to be administered on the other four days. He indicated that any change to the thyroid dosing would take at least six weeks to have any effect. With that, he sent us a blood requisition via email and set a follow-up appointment for the end of November.

During the month of November, Mina and I continued to watch our favourite TV game show, 'Jeopardy.' As we watched the show, we challenged each other to guess the correct questions to the answers. Sadly, on the November 8th program, the show's producer announced that beloved long-time host Alex Trebek had lost his battle with pancreatic cancer. We had lost a Canadian cultural icon. The show would never be the same without him.

Later in the month, we received the next set of blood tests ordered by Dr. Boright. Although Mina's glucose (A1C) level was high at 7.3%, all of the cholesterol tests came back within the normal ranges. The thyroid hormones, both the TSH and thyroxine (T4) were now in the normal range. Satisfied that the modified Synthroid dosing had worked, Dr. Boright scheduled a repeat of the tests within six months. He also noted that the annual ultrasound monitoring for the thyroid cancer tissue could be revised to be repeated every five years, due to the extremely low risk of reoccurrence of the disease. We both were relieved with the recent good news surrounding the test results. Myeloma patients and caregivers really need a regular dose of encouraging feedback, even if it is modest in nature.

# The Stamp Collector

During August 2020, we had several appointments with the hospital dental clinic. We met with Dr. Mardini who recommended new lower dentures for Mina. Apparently, the oral cancer surgery had affected the biomechanics of the jaw which resulted in an improper fit for the old dentures. My private medical insurance coupled with the government subsidy would cover most of the cost of the new dentures.

As I sat patiently recording the dental clinic procedure in my daily diary, Dr. Mardini took notice of my notes. He then asked me the same question that many of the other specialists had posed, "Are you an Engineer?" I replied that my expertise was in the area of budgeting and finance. However, during my career I did have extensive interactions with many engineers.

I noticed that engineering personality types tended to approach life in a very rigid, linear fashion and that they were quite anal retentive with focusing their attention on patterns. They tend to inhabit a very black and white world where everything, including medicine, can be reduced to a simple equation. I suppose that my daily diary which documented Mina's progress with neatly printed block letters evoked memories of frustrating interactions the doctors had with our engineering friends.

I could imagine an engineer patient caregiver inquiring about a specific therapy, making a computation and then arriving at a conclusion about a definite outcome. If an expected result failed to materialize, such as a stringent complete response to a cancer treatment, you could see how it would turn an engineer's world upside-down. It would be as if Newton's law of gravity was proven to be false or perhaps the speed of light could be exceeded, resulting in time travel.

Aside from his mischaracterization of my personality, Dr. Mardini seemed interested in my organizational skills. He asked me if I had any tips to help him organize his voluminous stamp collection. This was the first time I had met a devoted stamp collector. His collection from the past 35 years consisted of unique stamps from across the globe. Apparently, stamp collecting is one of the world's most popular hobbies, unlike running, which attracts a very small proportion of the population. In any event, I replied in jest that a fix for his collection could be had for a very modest consulting fee.

Dr. Mardini then proceeded to make an impression of Mina's lower jaw. The plan was to construct the new dentures from metal rather than plastic. Both materials have their advantages and disadvantages. One week later we returned to the clinic and Dr. Mardini fitted a wax model with no issues. The manufactured dentures arrived the following week. Mina was instructed to wear them continuously. She was instructed to start with just soft food and follow-up with a strict hygiene protocol. It took a few more appointments at the dental clinic to make minor adjustments before Mina finally had a proper fit.

# The VQ Lung Study

Concerned with Mina's ongoing elevated heart rate and shortness of breath, Dr. Bautista recommended a VQ lung study. On August 17th, 2020, we arrived at the Toronto General Hospital medical imaging department. The technicians briefly walked me through the procedure. I recorded the details in my trusted daily medical diary.

The first part of the test uses a ventilation (V) scan to measure air flow in the lungs. Pictures are taken at different angles using a special x-ray scanner. Mina wore a breathing mask over her nose and mouth to allow for the inhalation of a radioisotope gas. The second part of the test involves a perfusion (Q) scan to see where blood flows in the lungs. For the second test, they injected a radioisotope into Mina's vein. The entire procedure was completed within 45 minutes.

After we arrived home later that afternoon, I was surprised to find that the test results were available on the hospital patient portal. The results indicated 'a normal flow' which sounded reassuring. The report then went into some technical terminology. There were multiple small to medium sized unmatched perfusion defects bilaterally at the mid left lung and a small defect in the right upper lobe. This indicated a high probability of a PE (pulmonary embolism).

As I was scratching my head, trying to make sense of the test results, we received a telephone call from Dr. Delatorre, an associate of Dr. Reece. He said that Mina needed to report to the hospital emergency department immediately. Since there was evidence of two blood clots, Mina would require an intravenous infusion of a blood thinner medication. I responded that she was already on 81 mg low-dose Aspirin. The doctor then stated that she would need a medicine which was stronger than that. So much for my input as a blood clot specialist.

We hopped back into the car to make another 15-kilometre return trip downtown, checking in at the Mount Sinai Hospital emergency department at 6 p.m. Since it was a tiny emergency room and there were COVID-19 restrictions in place, I was instructed to wait outside the building. The wait seemed to be an eternity.

Two hours later, Mina emerged from emergency after being treated for the blood clots. The doctor gave her an injection of Enoxaparin (Lovenox), an anticoagulant, directly into her abdomen. We were given a prescription for the drug which Mina was instructed to self-inject daily for one week. It was just as painful for me to watch her inject the drug into her stomach as it was for her to receive it. Her abdomen turned completely black and blue.

Mina was then enrolled in the hospital's thrombosis program. We were provided an instruction manual which gave advice on how to spot a potential deep vein thrombosis (DVT) which is a blood clot in the leg. The nurse practitioner prescribed a pill form of the anticoagulant called Edoxaban (Lixiana) which Mina would have to take for life. They also instructed us to discontinue the daily low dose Aspirin. We would have to consult the clinic if Mina had any planned medical procedures since the side effects of the drug could involve uncontrolled bleeding. There is no known antidote for the drug.

A month later, we got a call from Dr. Abdulrehman from the thrombosis clinic. This was a routine follow-up to ensure there were no further blood clot issues. We reported no serious side effects such as bleeding, dark stool or swelling in the legs. The drug was not toxic to the kidneys and there were no dietary restrictions. Given that there were no symptoms, the doctor indicated to us that the blood clots had healed. A few months later, Mina was instructed to stop the Lixiana medication and was given a new anticoagulant called Apixaban (Eliquis). The drug is a better alternative for folks who have mild to moderate kidney disease.

# Mina's Everyday Life with Multiple Myeloma

Mina's physical and emotional temperament with multiple myeloma varied from day to day, constantly changing, like a rollercoaster. One day she would awaken, full of energy only to crash a few hours later. Some days would see her feeling sad and lonely, while other days she exhibited a life full of hope and positivity. Regardless of the ups and downs, on most days she experienced some degree of normalcy, always ready to face any challenge, including cancer.

Although she always maintained a positive attitude, there were times that she could not suppress negative feelings, especially when she was lying awake at night, when everyone else was asleep. During these moments, it allowed her to ponder her anxiety and reminisce about her extended family, who live so very far away, with nightly video chats her only point of contact with them.

Living with cancer is quite unnerving and scary. But her fears were often overcome by the support of myself, her spouse. I would try to take an approach based on facts and science when discussing the disease with her, tirelessly researching all of the latest developments in multiple myeloma. The scientific approach allowed both of us to engage in mindfulness, accepting the disease, while living a life in retirement together that emphasized as much quality as possible.

During Mina's intermittent periods of depression and sadness, even with the full support of myself, Mila and our mutual friends, it was difficult for her to witness them suffering and sharing the pain with her. She constantly wondered if the burden imposed would be too difficult to shoulder. From doctor's appointments, to blood tests and chemotherapy treatments, she worried about the impact on her loved ones, fearing that it would be exhausting and overwhelming. Eventually, Mina realized that by becoming a knowledgeable patient, with a very resourceful pair of caregivers, the dark clouds would disappear, bringing the brightness of the sun's warmth.

I always tried to impart words of wisdom to Mina, saying, "Cancer is not a sprint, but a really long marathon." With multiple myeloma, we encouraged each other to look upon it simply as a long-term chronic condition that can be treated, beaten back into submission and overcome. With this, the goal is not only to extend life but also to balance the cancer treatments to achieve a relatively good quality of life, for all of us.

At times, Mina experienced pain that left her with feelings of hopelessness and distress. Over time, she learned to accept this, knowing that this was mainly due to the side effects of treatment. She learned to be brave, realizing that enduring the tough medicine would bring her benefits. It was cancer that strengthened her spirituality and provided a window into understanding how deep her connection to God is. A threat to one's mortality tends to make one appreciate and value life more than ever. Having multiple myeloma resulted in the strengthening of bonds, especially with her significant other, Mila and our extended network of family and friends. The love and caring they have shown throughout Mina's ordeal, became the greatest gift to her, greater than any material gift imaginable.

Yes, Mina has the scars to show from this journey, from becoming bald after the stem cell transplants to being nauseous from the drug therapy. I like to consider these outcomes a 'well-earned badge of courage.' In fact, the physical assault on her body had made her stronger. The knowledge that medical technology for this disease is advancing at a rapid pace has filled her with feelings of hope and inspiration. Survival rates have increased exponentially, with some experts predicting a cure within ten years. Mina wrote a memo to both myself and Mila, saying, "Thank-you for being the absolute best caregivers one could hope for. Words alone can never truly express my sincere and heartfelt thanks to both of you, always giving me encouragement throughout my illness. I have been so blessed to have you both accompany on my journey."

# The Final Supper

On February 12, 2020, we had our annual Fast Friends dinner at the historic one-hundred-year-old Stone Cottage Pub in Scarborough. Mina could not attend with me since she had to avoid group restaurant settings like the plague. Much of our banter centred around the news about a new, mysterious virus that had emerged in Wuhan, China. Visions of the 2003 SARS outbreak came to mind as we recalled the deadly coronavirus that resulted in 39 deaths in Toronto, mainly in hospital settings.

During that time, Chinese restaurants in the area were unfairly boycotted. Toronto itself became somewhat stigmatized. When we travelled to Boston for the 2003 Boston Marathon, some of the folks in the city would give us a wide berth after they learned we were visitors from Toronto.

Toronto's initial SARS outbreak was traced back to a guest or guests who stayed at Hong Kong's Metropole Hotel in late February and caught the virus from an infected Chinese physician there. At the time, no one knew that a new disease had emerged in China, and hospital workers who treated the first patients were unaware of the need to protect themselves. As a result, SARS spread rapidly in hospitals and then to the community. After four months, the World Health Organization declared the end of the outbreak.

The Fast Friends ended the evening with the usual thanks that we had another year of comradery and running. Lynne, one of our awesome power-walkers, gave me a very nice running cap. I told her that Mina would don the hat in an upcoming event.

We had planned a trip to New York City to participate in the MMRF 12-hour endurance race in support of multiple myeloma research. I had not yet registered for the event, which was planned for October 2020, but had purchased first-class airplane tickets using the gift certificate that the Fast Friends gave us as a wedding present in 2015. Sadly, that race, along with every other competitive running race would ultimately be cancelled. The COVID-19 pandemic would turn life upside down, not only for Toronto, but across the world.

# Tom Brokaw's Myeloma Story

During the summer of 2019, after work, I went to the local bookstore to browse the health and medicine section, hoping to find some motivational books on multiple myeloma. There were quite a few publications of a scientific nature that caught my attention which I eventually deemed far too technical to be of value. I needed a book that Mina could read and get some positive motivation from the words written within the covers. And then I spotted the acclaimed journalist Tom Brokaw's book entitled 'A Lucky Life Interrupted : A Memoir of Hope.'

At first, I assumed that the book had been misplaced. However, after reading the introduction to the book, it seemed to be the down-to-earth readable story I was looking for. Tom was indeed diagnosed with multiple myeloma in 2013. One year later he announced that his cancer was in full remission. This is exactly the message of hope and inspiration that we needed. Much like myself, Tom Brokaw, in order to learn as much about multiple myeloma as I did, started to keep a journal which documented his struggle with the disease and the importance of caregiving support. I purchased the book and presented it to Mina when I returned home. She finished reading it within one day.

After Mina had read the book, it was my turn to immerse myself in Tom's memoir. It was a fascinating read, not in the sense that the book conveyed a detailed depiction of multiple myeloma. Tom's book instead provided an inspirational story that focused on his lucky life, filled with accounts of his experiences in his career in journalism tempered by celebrations his love of life with his family, friends, co-workers and celebrities. Prior to his diagnosis, Tom led extremely physically active lifestyle. His wife also ran in the New York City marathon, finishing a respectable time of four hours. The multiple myeloma diagnosis was a simple artifact or incidental event in their lives with which he faced with courage and determination.

In 2014, Tom conducted an interview with Louis Zamperini, the famous World War II veteran and Olympic distance runner. After his plane crashed into the ocean, he spent 47 days on a lifeboat, before being captured by the Japanese, who tortured and beat him mercilessly. He gained fame in the 1936 Berlin Olympics, finishing 8th in the 5,000-metre event, with an amazing final sprint lap of 56 seconds that even caught the attention of Adolf Hitler.

Angelina Jolie, who directed the film 'Unbroken' which profiled Zamperini's ordeal, commented to Tom on the resilience and strength of the human spirit. Zamperini himself said that it was only his eternal optimism allowed him to survive in a Japanese POW camp. He could tell simply by observing an individual's attitude, which of his fellow captors would survive and who would not.

I think multiple myeloma patients and their caregivers experience their own version of 'Unbroken.' They begin their journey with a diagnosis of multiple myeloma, evoking a sense of hopelessness after suddenly being cast out on a never-ending ocean. They are lucky enough to be given a lifeboat with the powerful myeloma treatments available today.

But the defining feature of myeloma survivors is reflected in their indomitable spirit and resilience. You may need drugs to thwart the physical impacts of the disease but there is no substitute for a positive attitude to help with that final 56 second sprint across the finish line. As Zamperini noted, psychological fortitude is the key ingredient in the promotion of healing and recovery.

Tom and his wife Meredith were shining examples of how a caregiving and advocacy team work together in perfect unison. They were indeed two sides of the same coin. Tom would look upon his myeloma diagnosis somewhat dispassionately while also taking on the advocacy portfolio. He would not hesitate to question the science behind his disease, seek second medical opinions or criticize the physician who failed to provide proper follow-up after a kyphoplasty procedure to help stabilize his spine.

Tom also provided a glimpse of some of the inadequacies inherent in the U.S. medical system. He was fortunate that his private medical insurance allowed him to receive the best possible care in some of the most renowned medical centres in the country. However, this high standard of care did not extend to huge portion of the population who did not have access to gold-plated medical insurance plans.

There were efforts made to correct this imbalance. For example, he maintained a friendship with Geraldine Ferraro, the former Vice-Presidential nominee, who was diagnosed with multiple myeloma, eventually succumbing to the disease after a twelve-year struggle. She went to Washington to successfully press in Congressional hearings for passage of the Hematological Cancer Research Investment and Education Act.

A portion of the Act created the Geraldine Ferraro Cancer Education Program, which directs the U.S. Secretary of Health and Human Services to establish an education program for patients of blood cancers and the general public. Ferraro became a frequent speaker on the disease. She was also an avid supporter and honorary board member of the Multiple Myeloma Research Foundation.

There is something about a personal diagnosis of a potentially fatal disease that often jump-starts a person into the role of advocacy and medical activism. Regarding my own situation with Mina's diagnosis, I could only dream to become a similar shining example of patient caregiving and advocacy exhibited by Tom, Meredith and Geraldine.

# 2016 : The World-Famous Houston Running Festival

Regarding the inequities of the U.S. medical system, I had my own first-hand experience as an ultra-runner. In December, 2016, I travelled to Texas to run a 50-mile event in the 'World-Famous Houston Running Festival.' It turned out to be a small, intimate event which took place on a two-mile loop in Bear Creek Park. I finished in second place overall in a time of 11:28, a far cry from my personal best performance of 7:33, but a satisfying run overall. I collected my finisher's medal, thanked the race organizers and then headed to my hotel to rest up until my flight back to Toronto the next day.

After showering, I headed to the hotel restaurant, limping gingerly, still feeling the after-effects of the 50-mile race on my leg muscles. I ordered my favourite veggie burger, fries and washed the meal down with two post-race celebration beers. Suddenly, a wave of nausea and dizziness swept over my entire body. I stood up, hoping to alleviate the condition, but immediately fainted, collapsing in a heap on the floor, narrowly avoiding hitting my head on the table.

Another restaurant patron witnessed my demise and came over to assist me. I quickly regained consciousness and was able to sit down, trying to make sense of what just transpired. He immediately called for an ambulance, although I was lucid enough to indicate that it was not necessary. As a runner, I recognized the signs of major dehydration, having been in similar situations in previous running events. Apparently, the transition from cold weather running in Toronto to the warm, humid conditions in Texas was too abrupt a change for my body to adapt to. I should have known better.

The ambulance attendants arrived in very short order along with the John, the manager of the hotel, who happened to be French-Canadian. Upon learning that I was also from Canada, he asked me in French if I could speak the language. Although I had lost most of my French language skills, I was able to respond with, "Enchanté de faire votre connaissance." (A pleasure to meet you). I apologized for my pronunciation, but he said that it was perfect. I suppose the brain has a unique system for long-term memory recall, despite years of second-language inactivity.

The two EMT's that attended to me were really friendly and insisted I be placed in the back of the ambulance for evaluation. I indicated that it was really not required since I was already feeling recovered from my ordeal. When they learned that I had just run fifty miles, they exclaimed, "You must be crazy!" After some cajoling, I reluctantly agreed and they transported me via a stretcher to the ambulance.

The plan was to take me to a local hospital for treatment, to which I immediately objected. "I don't have medical insurance coverage in the States. How much would this cost me out-of-pocket?" I learned that it would cost anywhere from a minimum of $10,000 and up, depending on the length of stay required. Bear in mind, this cost represented the co-pay required, even for an individual who had private medical insurance. Upon hearing this, I told them that there was absolutely no way that they were going to take me to the hospital!

When they learned that I was from Canada, they said, "I hear you have socialized medicine in Canada. Everything is free, right?" I responded with, "It isn't exactly a free service. Take a look at my income tax bill and compare it to what you pay!" I was not complaining about Canada's 'socialized' system. I was only too happy to pay more taxes to support a government-run system that would be there when I needed it, regardless of the cost.

Mina's treatment for multiple myeloma was a case in point. From the start of her diagnosis right through the induction therapy, stem cell transplants, maintenance drugs and monitoring, I took an estimated tally of the costs, that thankfully we did not have to pay. It came to a staggering $2 million dollars and counting! I then imagined how a low-to-modest income earner in the States could possibly manage to cope with their illness, without having adequate medical insurance. There simply would not be any options available. Thank God for individual efforts like we saw with Geraldine Ferraro's initiative to make a dent in the health-care system!

The ambulance attendants agreed not to transport me to the hospital but they first wanted to check my vitals and ask me a series of skill-testing questions to ensure my cognitive abilities remained intact. "Who is the President of the United States?", was the very first question. That was a bit of a trick question since the 2016 election had just been held the month previously. I replied, "Technically, it is Barack Obama with President-elect Donald Millhouse Trump set to take office next January."

They laughed at my reply and said, "Very good. But you got Donald Trump's middle name wrong." I said with a shrug, "Oh yes, I had him confused with Richard Nixon. They seem to be two birds of a feather!" They took this with the good humour with which the remark was intended, giving me a high-five. However, I was concerned at the time that the incorrect answer might jeopardize my situation or that they were possibly Donald Trump supporters, being from the red state of Texas. In the end, they merely asked me to sign a waiver to indicate that I had refused medical treatment at the hospital. When I returned to Canada, I kept worrying that somehow a huge bill would arrive in the mail for the one-hour ambulance service. Thankfully, that did not materialize!

# The Toronto Multiple Myeloma Support Group

On October 5th, 2019, we attended a myeloma support group meeting. The meetings are held every other month in a local church meeting room. We found that the opportunity to meet with other myeloma patients and caregivers was quite inspirational. Some of the support group members were long-term survivors while others were just like us, starting out in uncharted territory. There were also free educational materials, refreshments and guest speakers who gave presentations on a wide variety of topics.

The guest speaker at this meeting was our wonderful nurse practitioner Suzanne Rowland from the Princess Margaret Hospital. Her presentation topic was entitled 'Management of Side Effects and Supportive Care.' We were keen to listen, learn and ask questions. Prior to Suzanne's presentation, I was relying primarily on getting information on side effects from Dr. Google. Although the internet has a wealth of material relating to the impact of myeloma treatment on the patient's quality of life, it can lead you down a pathway to depression and anxiety if you treat it as the gospel. It is always best to consult your medical team first.

During the question-and-answer session, I noted that there was an inquiry concerning the free light chains and the calculation of the kappa to lambda ratio. The questioner wanted to know how it is possible to have an abnormal value for the kappa and lambda light chains but still have a normal ratio calculated. I had often pondered that very same issue since I noted that Mina's free light chain calculations sometimes would show this apparent contradiction.

Suzanne did not really have a good explanation for this since ratio calculations were not in her wheelhouse. After the meeting, I decided to test out my own hypothetical values of kappa and lambda to determine if I could solve the puzzle. Sure enough, I found that if the values were just outside the normal range, the result would often be a normal ratio.

If you have ever read the book 'How to Lie with Statistics' authored by Darrell Huff in 1954, you can see the potential for statistical calculations to distort reality! Robert Giffen, in 1892, wrote in the Economic Journal stated, "There are liars, there are outrageous liars, and there are scientific experts." We can conclude that the misuse of statistical data can lead to a serious mis-interpretation of the results.

One important tidbit that Suzanne did convey was that data for a single point in time is not a very good indicator of treatment effectiveness. If you are going to review the laboratory test results for your loved one's myeloma, look for the trend-line over a longer period of time. For example, at one point during maintenance therapy, Mina's free light chain lambda, the cancer marker, was measured at 60, almost 35 points above the normal level. But the kappa to lambda ratio was normal.

After a consultation with Dr. Reece, we decided to wait until we had the chance to review the results of future blood tests. After reviewing multiple data points, the numbers were consistently at the same level. The disease had stabilized and only a minor tweak to one of the maintenance drugs, increasing the Ninlaro to 3 mg, was required. We also decided to discontinue the monthly Zometa bone strengthening therapy since it was hurting Mina's kidney function. Instead, a monoclonal antibody drug, Denosumab, would be administered by Mina's family doctor every six months. Although this drug is mainly prescribed to alleviate osteoporosis symptoms, there is some evidence that it could help reduce the risk of bone fractures and perhaps repair the bone damage that is a trademark feature of multiple myeloma.

I also asked Suzanne about the new technology involving next generation genomic sequencing and minimal residual disease (MRD) testing. The new gold standard in myeloma disease monitoring is defined by the ability to detect one myeloma cancer cell out of one million cells. If the MRD tests reveal no detectable cancer within the sample, it would indicate a MRD negative status which is a particularly good remission. This is important to determine how well the patient is responding to a specific treatment and also to make informative decisions on how precision medicine therapy may be directed against specific genetic mutations. In the end, Suzanne seemed to indicate that the new testing would be available at the Princess Margaret Hospital.

At a later Myeloma Support Group meeting, we had the pleasure of meeting Munira Premji, one of the Executive Committee members of the Toronto Myeloma Support Group and author of the book 'Choosing Hope: One Woman. Three Cancers.' Her story is remarkably similar to Mina's battle with cancer. Munira is a survivor of three advanced cancers : Non-Hodgkin Lymphoma, Multiple Myeloma and Breast Cancer, all diagnosed within a few years of each other.

We were so inspired by her energetic spirit and positive outlook on life that we purchased her book. The cover page has a sub-title that reads 'A Story of Inspiration, Resilience and Courage.' In my view, these are three essential qualities that define how a myeloma patient's attitude can play a pivotal role in overcoming this disease. As Louis Zamperini once said, "In a prisoner-of-war camp, the complainers all die early. Whatever situation I find myself in, attitude has a healing effect on the body."

I must admit, prior to my experience as a multiple myeloma patient caregiver and advocate, I had been quite skeptical of claims that the mind can have a miraculous healing effect on the body. Perhaps I had possessed the rigid mindset that required hard scientific proof of this concept. I credit my supplemental studies in psychology, specifically physiological psychology, for setting my thinking straight.

It was the documented scientific evidence of the placebo effect that convinced me that the intricate web of neurons firing in our brains produce more than a mere conscious awareness of our own existence. One's attitudes and expectations can and do shape our body's response to disease. Positive mental vibes can play a key role in producing measurable bio-chemical reactions that can promote healing and thwart cancer. Although we all have this ability, some folks are more successful than others at tapping into it. Our brains essentially create our own reality rather than merely processing sensory input from the outside world.

On December 7, 2019, Dr. Mary Elliot, an Assistant Professor of Psychiatry and a clinical investigator at the Princess Margaret Cancer Centre, presented 'The Role of Mindfulness in Supporting People with Myeloma' at our Toronto Myeloma Support Group meeting. Her talk reminded me of the healing power of mental conditioning. We have much more than just drug therapies available in our arsenal of weapons to fight multiple myeloma. There is a very complex and powerful machine inside our skulls that we have at our disposal. Alia Crum, a psychologist at Stanford stated "I don't think the power of mind is limitless," she said. "But I do think we don't yet know where those limits are."

In her opening, Dr. Elliot described a time when she went for a walk on a nature trail, hoping to get a photograph of a beautiful monarch butterfly. She spotted plenty of the creatures but was unable to have the opportunity to capture a still photo of any of them. Just as she was about to give up, she by chance looked down, focused and unexpectedly found a fifty-dollar bill, which she promptly donated to charity.

Dr. Elliot then went on to explain that sometimes when we focus on looking for what we want, we tend to miss what's here. In summary, she explained that mindfulness involves a purposeful focus of attention with an underlying attitude that allows us not to judge our experience but to be curious about our experience. We don't necessarily have to like our experience, especially if it involves a cancer diagnosis, but 'showing up' for our experience implies that we can respond to it. The mindfulness approach employs the use of cognitive behavioural therapy, a technique which has been scientifically validated in clinical practice.

During the question-and answer-session, one audience member asked Dr. Elliot, "We know that mindfulness improves one's quality of life. However, do you have any evidence that mindfulness therapy directly attacks the myeloma?" She responded by saying that she was not aware of any evidence which supported that conjecture. However, Dr. Elliot mused that it would be an interesting area for future research. In theory, one could conduct a clinical trial comparing the treatment outcomes of a group who received only the myeloma drug therapy with a group who also had mindfulness training added as part of the program. It would be relatively easy to measure the body's immune system response between the two experimental groups.

It is my personal unscientific opinion that a holistic integrative approach which recruited the power of the mind would not only result in a subjective improvement in one's quality of life, but would also activate the body's bio-chemical processes through a placebo effect. Science has already determined that an activation of neural pathways in the brain leads to the release of a variety of substances such as serotonin, endorphins, dopamine and adrenaline. Everyone has heard of the 'runner's high.' I have had the good fortune of experiencing this phenomenon after a very intense race or training run. You don't have to engage in physical exercise to achieve this effect. An individual's expectations can also drive the release of this bio-chemical cascade.

Just before the COVID-19 pandemic shut down our in-person myeloma support group meetings, we attended one final gathering that was in a 'meet and greet' format. Everyone would be seated in a big circle. The meeting's moderator would go around the circle asking each person to give a brief introduction and relate their own personal myeloma story.

When it came to my turn, I simply expressed how inspirational the support group meetings have been. Listening to the other patients and caregivers was very educational. Since Mina and I were 'newbies', we gleaned invaluable information from the other support group members, some of whom had been dealing with the disease for several years. We suddenly did not feel totally alone, fighting a cancer that we had absolutely no familiarity with. The interactions with the others offered hope that this was a treatable disease for which survival rates had increased exponentially in just the last five years.

Mina's speech was still somewhat compromised from the oral cancer surgery. She did comment on the stem cell transplant procedure and highly recommended choosing the hospital in-patient option as opposed to the outpatient protocol. Of course, this stimulated a fierce debate with the folks who preferred the outpatient approach, which consisted of daily trips to the hospital, with recuperation within the comfort and convenience of their own homes.

Each of these two options have pros and cons. The outpatient procedure simply would not have been feasible for Mina. She was in the high-risk category. The majority of her hospital stay consisted of being hooked up 24/7 to an intravenous line receiving hydration and anti-viral medications. The outpatient option would have introduced a greater level of risk. The hospital staff were constantly on the lookout for serious infections or side effects from the treatment.

# 2013 Fort Clinch 100-Miler : An Extended Period of Morning

Our workplace had an employee fitness centre which allowed me to go for a refreshing 8-kilometre lunch-time run. I could run for 50 minutes, through downtown and along the waterfront. It is amazing how a vigorous run can re-energize you and clear your brain of any fog. Often, while running, I would come up with innovative solutions to a work-related project. It seemed like the extra oxygen intake provided an energy burst that sparked creative insights.

One day, while getting ready for my run, I overheard a fellow runner remarking about the recent loss of a loved one to cancer. He said, "With today's advancements in medical technology and treatment options, this has only provided for an extended period of mourning." Reflecting back on that moment, I have come to realize that he was viewing his loss through a very pessimistic lens.

Disease, illness and suffering are all part of the human experience. I believe that my colleague's pessimistic view of the world arises whenever a turn of events reminds us of our own mortality, perhaps vicariously when a cancer diagnosis strikes close to home. Speaking from first-hand experience, I also went through all of the various stages from denial right up to acceptance.

You as a patient caregiver and advocate have the choice to decide how you will react. Once you get past the shock and denial, it is essential to make it your mission to see your new role through a scientific lens. Science has given us a golden gift in the form of not only extending the lifespan of your loved one, but vastly improving their quality of life. Once you are able to grasp this more optimistic view of the world, the patient caregiving role becomes much more meaningful and less daunting.

This is why I think that my colleague's phrase should be re-worded as an 'extended period of morning.' To borrow a cliché, there is light at the end of the tunnel that becomes brighter as the sun rises over the horizon. This brightness comes in the form of new research that results in exciting new discoveries and medical advancements towards a cancer cure. Nowhere is this more evident than in the ongoing progress being made in the treatment options available for multiple myeloma patients.

We can extend the analogy of the extended morning to ultra running events that last for 24 hours or more. Only a small fraction of the running community, including yours truly, are mad enough to participate in these extreme running events. For the first few hours, you may be running full of energy, feeling that you are invincible and can go on forever.

As the day progresses and darkness slowly settles around you, there is only your inner thoughts, physical sensations of muscle pain and a flashlight to light your way down the forest path. You may trick yourself that you cannot possibly take another step, that you should drop out now and that it is pointless to continue. It would be easy simply to surrender to your feelings and give up.

Suddenly, after twenty hours of running, the sun starts to rise over the horizon. After running for more than twenty hours, you realize that you are only a few hours away from crossing the finish line. As dawn turns into daylight, things become brighter, both literally and figuratively. The extended period of morning engulfs you. You finish the race feeling like a true champion. Nothing can defeat you, not even cancer.

I entered the Fort Clinch 100-mile race in Florida with excitement and anticipation of experiencing again a huge physical and psychological endurance effort rewarded by the morning sun shining brightly on me at the end. This race was an opportunity to restore my shaken confidence after my failure to complete the Winter Beast of Burden 100-mile race in January. It also to serve as a training race for the 24-Hour World Championships in the Netherlands, in which I would be competing as a member of the Canadian team.

One week earlier, I had arrived at the start line of the Hamilton 30-km Around the Bay Race (ATB). This was my 12th year running this event. It was intended to be a great tune-up race to get my aerobic system accustomed to faster-paced running. It was good timing too since it was so close to the Fort Clinch 100-Mile race.

Pre-race, while standing in the long line for the urinals, I met our Canadian Team Manager, Armand, who was also running in the race. He thanked me for joining the team and I replied "Looking forward to the challenge!" There were only four men on the team that year, but there were eight women who qualified, which I thought was great. Women runners tend to do relatively better than their male counterparts in ultra distance races.

Due to my above-average performances in previous ATB races, I was assigned a position just behind the elite runners at the start line. I met a few of my ultra running friends at the start, including Jack and Steve (who had placed 2nd in the 100-Mile Winter Beast of Burden in January). I shook their hands and wished them well in their race. I lined up with the 2-hour and 15-minute pace bunny, because I really had no time goal for this race and just wanted some company along the route. To make a long story short, the rabbit was perfect in his pacing and we ran exactly 45 minutes for three consecutive 10-km segments. I crossed the finish line inside the stadium in 2:15, and then collected my medal and post-race food.

I then drove back to Toronto, and headed to the airport to catch my flight to Arizona, where I planned to do some hiking in the Santa Rita mountains near my former place in Green Valley. The plane was one hour late taking off since the pilot had to 'test' the left engine prior to departure. This announcement didn't exactly give me a warm and fuzzy feeling inside. But I did have the bulkhead seat with plenty of room to stretch out and review my safety plan for bailing out if there was a problem. Of course, when you hit the ground at 500 m.p.h., I figured that knowing how to use the flotation cushion would not be of too much value.

The plane arrived in Phoenix, Arizona on time since the pilot made up for the lost time during the flight. As Seinfeld once said, "Geez, if they can fly the plane faster, why not just do that all the time?" My flight to Tucson was not until the next morning at 7 a.m. and so I wandered over to the last cafeteria open in the airport, stood in line and ordered a grilled cheese sandwich. The cashier yelled back to the cooks "One grilled cheese sandwich walking in."

Sadly, the cooks replied that they were now closed and no more sandwiches were being made. Starving and with no snacks in my baggage, I just sat down at one of the tables. A few minutes later, the manager came over and apologized for not being able to serve me. She offered me this cheese pizza that someone ordered but did not pick up and was just about ready to go into the garbage. I accepted the free pizza garbage and greedily inhaled it. She came back later and offered some more free stuff from the kitchen, but the pizza just about did me in and I was not in the mood for any more food.

It was close to midnight and so I made my way over to my boarding gate for the next morning's flight to Tucson. I found an empty row of seats and settled in for a good night's sleep (NOT!). I got on the regional jet flight to Tucson, we taxied for 45 minutes and then had a 20-minute flight. I picked up my rental car in Tucson, listened to the sales agent warnings about the need to purchase extra insurance, GPS and the like, which doubled the price of my four-day car rental. After driving for 20 minutes, I arrived at my place in Green Valley. I managed to get some real sleep, resting up for the next day's hike to the top of Mount Wrightson.

It was always my goal to hike to the top of the highest mountain in the Santa Rita range. I can see it from my doorstep and it seemed like a good way to get some extra exercise and altitude training prior to the Fort Clinch 100-miler. After a 20-km drive to the trailhead at Madera Canyon, I started my hiking adventure! I met several experienced hikers along the way, mostly senior citizens who were well-equipped with the latest hiking poles.

It was an 8-km trip up 'Old Baldry' trail to the top of Mount Wrightson. After only 1-km, I came across two beautiful deer grazing on the trail in front of me. They spotted me but did not really pay me too much attention. I suppose animals instinctively know the humans who are good and not a threat to them. Their heads certainly would make a lovely souvenir trophy, but I really had to get on with my trek up the mountain. I didn't want to get caught on the trail after dark since the Coronado Forest is also home to black bears and mountain lions.

After three hours, I made it to the summit! I signed the registry book and wrote a little poem about my experience as an inspiration-warning to others who were bold enough to follow in my footsteps. It only took me two hours to descend back to the trailhead. I was now energized for my 100-mile race!

A few days later, I returned to the Tucson airport at 11 p.m. My flight to Houston and Jacksonville, Florida was not until early the next morning. I found a comfy sofa in the airport lounge to bed down for the night. I really appreciated the Mayor of Tucson greeting over the PA every five minutes, extolling the virtues of Tucson as a great place to visit, and nicknamed 'Science City.'

I got up from the sofa at 4 a.m. and stood in line at the security checkpoint and then proceeded to my boarding gate. After switching planes in Houston, I arrived in Jacksonville on time. I picked up the car rental and drove twenty-five miles north to Amelia Island to pick up my race kit and number at the Red Otter store. I returned later to the store for the pizza dinner and meet some of the other ultra runners. I had a chance to talk with the 2011 race winner, Bruce Choi, who said that only three runners finished that year since the race was held in the middle of summer in 100-degree heat. Apparently, several runners ended up in hospital that year. Cool! If you can't take the heat, stay out of the kitchen!

Upon returning to the hotel to get some much-needed sleep, I could not sleep a wink, tossing and turning all night. I finally arose at 4 a.m. and started prepping my feet with bandages to help prevent blister formation.

At the race start, Caleb, the race director delayed the start to 6:30 a.m. to allow more daylight and give the runners more prep time. And then we lined up and he gave a 10-second count down and we were off! I ran with the lead group which included mostly young pups like Bruce, Taryn, Crystal and others who were not part of my generation but were fun to talk with.

The race course was a 10-mile (16-km) trail loop that you had to complete ten times to get the 100 miles within a thirty-hour time limit. The trail was rolling, no really steep hills but it was a total of 9,000 feet in elevation gain and loss over the 10 loops. I stayed on a 20-hour finish time for the first 100-km. The final 60-km were pure torture since both my feet became totally blistered from the trail running. I applied some lubricant at the start-finish but that turned out to be only marginally effective. It was the most uncomfortable 60-km I ever ran/shuffled in my life. The twenty-hour time goal was not going to happen.

There was also a very long concrete pier that we had to run out and back on every time before returning to the start / finish area. It was really annoying since it was narrow and we had to avoid people who were fishing off the pier throughout the race. There was also a short loop around an alligator swamp that made me nervous running at night. I enjoyed running on the beach area around Fort Clinch, which was about 800 meters of mostly hard-packed sand. The cool breeze was welcome since it was hot during the day and I noticed serious amounts of salt accumulating on my running shirt. On my final loop at about 4 a.m., there was a Sunday Easter service inside Fort Clinch. I heard them praying to Jesus to help them make it through one more day. I thought to myself, "try running one-hundred miles and have a real religious experience."

Under the bright morning sunshine, I headed to the finish line and picked up the pace, ignoring all of the blisters and body issues, just thankful that I was going to make it and celebrate another 100-miler. I crossed the finish line in 6th place overall in 25-hours and 13-minutes. They got a perfect photo of me with the time clock and Caleb awarded me the 100-mile finisher's belt buckle! Only 50% of the roughly thirty starters finished the race, a shockingly low finish percentage! The Fort Clinch race motto reads 'Nothing Great is Easy.' So true, whether you are a runner or a patient caregiver!

# Dealing with Loss

After I returned home, I read a very moving race report from the overall winner of the Fort Clinch 100-mile race, former national champion Dave James. It was a story about Dave's inspiration for returning to Florida. His fiancée had successful chemotherapy for cancer back in 2004. The doctors were excited that she would beat the odds. They gave their blessing for the couple to take a week in Florida where they had both vacationed together before.

However, the weekend of The Fort Clinch 100 was scheduled on the tenth-year anniversary of the last trip that Dave and his fiancée would take. Just before their trip, the doctors had informed the couple that her cancer had not only returned but metastasized to her lungs, spine, and brain. In 2004, they visited the beach in Cape May, New Jersey, had their last meal together and made love for the last time. Dave would return to Florida often to mourn, remember her, and run. In 2005, 2006, 2007, and 2008 Dave returned to the Space Coast, Gulf Coast, and Disney to race and heal his soul.

After reading Dave's story, of course, I was at first reduced to tears. But Dave's account of his loved one's initial victory and then struggle with relapsed cancer, is a perfect example of hope, resilience and inspiration. It was truly an extended period of morning, as Dave emerged stronger than ever, performing as a true champion, even after experiencing the heart-breaking loss of a loved one. Dave was a champion both in terms of his running accomplishments and his role as a supportive caregiver, who always gave one-hundred percent, never giving up. His story was never an extended period mourning, but a lesson in strength of character, despite the odds.

I had come across other 'periods of morning' earlier in life, among friends and co-workers. During my career at the City of Toronto, my former Director, Ross Cuthbert, had suddenly been diagnosed with advanced stage colon cancer. Despite aggressive surgical interventions and chemotherapy, sadly he passed away in November, 1999. He had given advance instructions not to have a traditional funeral. He opined that funerals were too depressing. But he did write his own obituary just days before his passing. It read as follows:

My Friends,

Forgive me for leaving the party early. I have chosen not to have a standard funeral or a formal viewing because these would not be happy events - and I insist on leaving the world the same way I have tried to live in it - with smiles, joy and goodwill. My death is sad but not tragic because I have had a rich life. I have laughed, cried, loved and been loved, enjoyed the company of friends and lived life to the fullest extent that I could. I have lived longer than expected and survived against the odds to find romance, love and above all, to witness the birth and development of my two little miracles - Brittany and Yardley.

Who would have believed it possible 30 years ago? I have treasured the many and varied friends I have had at my side throughout my journey. There are no words to express my gratitude, to repay you all for the love and comradeship, the support given so freely - no words to even say a proper 'thanks' just for being a friend. I will miss you.

But I have had yet another gift lately - the time to visit, call or talk to as many of my friends and family as possible. Let these happy contacts serve as my goodbyes to you all. My family will be saying goodbye to me privately on the Scarborough Bluffs - one of our favourite places to be together, to walk and find peace. Please remember me in a similar fashion.

Remember the good times, the laughs we had, the special times we all shared. No greater tribute could I request. I leave asking but one last favour. Cathy, Brittany and Yardley will be beyond my protection and I will be unable to supply the hugs and kisses that they all need. Please remember them and love them as you would your own family - they will need good friends at every step of their life's journey. My love to you all - may you walk life's journey in good health, with friends at your side and a smile on your face.

Ross Cuthbert - November 1999.

There were many times in the past where I considered giving up the fight by just assuming that nature, destiny or extreme bad luck was to blame for Mina's fight with three different cancers. I could have easily succumbed to my emotions, by giving up on running and life in general. Whenever these thoughts entered my mind, I always remembered that life is a never-ending series of challenges, with the fight against cancer being just a tiny blip on the radar screen.

Being a competent patient caregiver requires the recruitment of both your psychological and physical resources, much like an ultra runner struggling to complete a 100-mile race. No matter how much time you and your significant other spend together, it is simply never enough. Remember, you are not mourning for your loved one. Rather, you are spending an extended period of morning with your loved one, an inseverable bond that grows stronger in the light of day.

# 2007 : The Creemore Vertical Challenge

During the summer of 2007, I competed in the inaugural 50-km Creemore Vertical Challenge. The reference to 'vertical' in the race name is an understatement. The race was held on a combination of steep back country roads, with some uphill trail sections thrown in for variety. Holding the event in the middle of summer, with sweltering heat and humidity, added an even greater level of masochism to it.

The race was organized by Pierre and his wife Lee Anne, local community icons and fellow ultra-marathon runners. Pierre would be renowned for his cultivation of Canadian maple syrup every Fall. Lee Anne played an integral part in the event, crafting home-made clay finisher medallions and trophies. I still cherish the giant-sized coffee mug that provides the vessel for my morning java.

Although trail running is definitely not my forte, I do enjoy competing in these races, if only to count the number of face plants and ankle twists that inevitably come my way. The race commenced in front of Pierre and Lee Anne's country home, which backs onto the Mad River, south of Creemore, Ontario. One of the event organizers starts the race with a blast from a 12-guage shotgun.

The course consists of a 25-km loop that is repeated twice, just in case you needed to be reminded how grueling the first loop was. As the race started, I was quickly left in the dust by some of the more talented trail blazers. After completing the first loop, I was really tempted to throw in the towel, call it a day and head for the beer casket that Pierre provided as a reward to the weary runners. But I resisted the urge to quit and pressed on.

During the second loop, to my surprise, I had caught up to some of the lead runners, who were running on empty and would eventually drop out of the race. One of the competitors who was initially well ahead of me, Jim Orr, looked over his shoulder and spotted me tailing behind him. After twisting my ankle on a flat section of country road, he encouraged me not to give up.

Eventually, the pain in my ankle resolved itself and we continued running together, over hill and dale. With approximately ten kilometres remaining, Jim asked me, "How about we tie this race?" This was a great relief to me since I knew that Jim could have easily outran me to the finish line, being a more talented 50-km runner than myself. We crossed the finish line with exactly the same finishing time of 4:32:44.

After several years, Pierre and Lee Anne finally ended the Creemore Vertical Challenge race. It was disappointing to the ultra running crowd, but understandable. Organizing any race event takes a tremendous commitment in terms of obtaining legal permits, rounding up a small army of volunteers to provide assistance, setting up the course and arranging the awards ceremony.

On September 24, 2020, the ultra running community received some very sad news. Lee Anne had suddenly passed away after a short bout with advanced lung cancer. Pierre and Lee Anne had just returned home from a hiking and tourist adventure in Portugal. Lee Anne had returned to her rigorous training program, which she had 'reduced' from running 150-km down to 80-km per week after experiencing shortness of breath when running up 4-kilometre hills. In 2015, Lee Anne had broken the 100-mile record for her age category, running for 26 hours and 34 minutes, with only three 4-minute breaks. Lee Anne also briefly held the road 12-hour world record for women 60-64 years of age.

The COVID-19 pandemic made it difficult to arrange a doctor's appointment. When they were finally able to get a chest x-ray, the results were not encouraging. Lee Anne received one session of chemotherapy before passing away shortly thereafter. The news was not only sad, but shocking since she had been a vegetarian and never smoked in her life. As Pierre noted in his blog, 'One of her oncologists had stated, cancer is not overly discriminating.' A memorial fun run would be scheduled to honour Lee Anne. I will certainly be there to celebrate her life.

# COVID-19 : Living in Interesting Times

"Better to be a dog in times of tranquility than a human in times of chaos." (寧為太平犬

，不做亂世人)　　　　　　　　　　　- Chinese idiom

After a one year pause from competing in races, due to all of the turmoil surrounding Mina's multiple myeloma diagnosis, on March 1, 2020, I ran the Chilly Half Marathon with my running partner Olex. He achieved a new personal best finish time of 1:47, while I finished with a personal worst performance of 1:51. Regardless of the results, it felt great to get back into racing. We took advantage of the free beer and chilly after the race at one of the local restaurants. Little did we know it would be the final in-person race event for the year before the COVID-19 pandemic scuttled all running events for the foreseeable future. Restaurant dining would also become a thing of the past.

Prior to the declaration of the national health emergency, we along with many others, had registered for several running events, including the Around the Bay 30-km race, the Sulphur Springs 50-miler, and the Niagara 100-km. Obviously, holding an event with throngs of runners packed together would be a really bad idea. It would be the perfect petri-dish environment for the virus to flourish. We received emails that the races were cancelled. In some cases, registration fees were refunded or we could choose a deferral to run at a later date once the pandemic was over. But runners, like myeloma patients, are a resilient group. We developed a saying, "There's no such thing as a tough pandemic, only soft runners."

The week after the Chilly Half Marathon in March, Olex and I did another Saturday morning long training run of 50-km. We returned to the YMCA to do a post-run stretch and relax before heading back home. I overheard many of the other gym members talking about the new

COVID-19 virus and how 'the world has suddenly been turned upside down.' I added my two cents by stating, "Yeah, people are just going crazy, hoarding toilet paper and hand sanitizers."

At that time, my only impression was it was going to be a short-lived panic and life would soon return to normal. Well, I was certainly in for a rude awakening. The very next day, a national health emergency was declared, people were ordered to stay at home and we were in a lockdown. The YMCA, my daily beacon of health and fitness would be closing its doors immediately, until further notice.

I sent an email to Olex requesting his input on maintaining our weekly long-run. I suggested that we continue with the training runs since there were no restrictions against going outside for a run. The advantage with running (or walking) is that one does not require a gym to do it. Although I enjoyed doing some mid-week workouts on the indoor track at the YMCA, running outside in the fresh air is always an attractive alternative.

We continued with our Saturday morning long runs, always practicing physical distancing from each other and from other folks who were sharing the same park pathway. During the weekdays, I would also get outside for some shorter 22-km runs in my local neighbourhood. The City of Toronto set up some 'quiet streets' as part of an initiative to encourage physical activity during the pandemic.

As part of the COVID-19 safety protocols, I tried wearing a face mask while running, but it soon became impossible to breathe once the mask became soaked with moisture. This was only a minor issue since I could easily avoid contact with other people by giving them extra space to pass by on the sidewalk or by simply running on the shoulder of the road. I was more concerned about getting bit by an unleashed dog than contracting the COVID virus.

Olex and I were quite disappointed with the cancellation of the Niagara 100-km race. Not to be thwarted, we decided to organize our own two-person 100-km event, to be held on May 30, 2020. By April, we had increased our weekend long-run to 60 kilometres to get our cardio system and running muscles primed for the big event. Mina's friend Mila would stay with Mina while I was out running all day.

I mapped out the course which began at my home in North Toronto, proceeded mostly on bike trails for fifty kilometres, returning along the Lake Ontario waterfront, with a finish back at my place. My running friends Mike and Melanie's home happened to be at the 71-kilometre point and so they offered us a water station stop on their doorstep. We gratefully accepted the assistance since our hydration backpacks and two water bottles would not last for the entire distance. The hydration backpacks were extremely useful. We had a full 2.5 litres plus two water bottles and we still ran short of fluid after 60-km.

The weather was perfect for running, with a breezy day that called for long sleeves and/or a light jacket. We started from my home, ran through the hydro corridor trail, and then into Scarborough, turning around at the Ajax Waterfront trail. By the halfway point, we both were running out of gas just as the sun came out from behind the clouds, adding some heat stress to our weary bodies. After munching on some protein energy bars, we recovered our momentum and continued with our 100-km quest. Although we ran together, my training partner and I maintained physical distancing between ourselves and other people during the run.

We followed the waterfront trail back through Pickering and then straight to Mike and Melanie's home, where they provided a water aid station. We then refilled our bladders (the ones attached to our hydration backpack, not the biological ones). Olex had run out of water about seven kilometres before that.

Mike then gave us pacing support through Thompson Park. His fresh legs gave us inspiration to continue with our quest to conquer the 100-km. We completed the run in a blistering time of 13-hours and 53 minutes, within the 14-hour cut-off for the official Niagara race. There were no medals for our finish, but I dedicated the achievement in spirit to Mina, who had endured exponentially more pain through her cancer treatments than I ever did through any of my running events.

With no in-person race events available during COVID-19, I registered to run a virtual 'Remembrance Day Half Marathon' in November 2020. At first, I was hesitant to run a virtual event since I was unsure if I could motivate myself to do a solo race effort. Typically, runners benefit from racing with other runners since it is easier to hold a faster pace in a live running race by feeding off of the energy of your fellow competitors.

Becoming restless with the COVID lockdowns, I decided to throw caution to the wind or as they say in Chinese 豁出去. I plotted a 21.1-km route from my home, hit the start button on my trusty Garmin GPS watch and let it rip. The spirit of the run was to commemorate our war heroes, particularly my father who risked his life as a British soldier during World War II.

As I ran through the local roads, avoiding the neighborhood dogs and machine gun fire, I paid tribute to all the brave heroes who landed at Juno Beach. I also visualized my father, running through the German countryside, rapid firing his Sten gun, mowing down the enemy before he was wounded by a German mortar shell.

It is amazing how a runner's cardio system instantly recognizes race pace, even during a solo effort. I ran at a brisk 4:47 per kilometre pace from the outset. The final 500 metres was an uphill climb on the local hydro corridor trail. After reaching exactly 21.1 kilometres, I stopped, pressed the save button on my GPS watch and did a one-kilometre cooldown walk back home.

I surprised myself with a finish time of 1:44, seven minutes faster than the Chilly Half Marathon that I had run several months earlier. With my first virtual race in the books, I uploaded the data and my running route, which was then sent to the race organizers for inclusion in the final results.

I ended up in sixth place overall out of a total of one hundred competitors. Not bad for a senior citizen. A few weeks later, I received a beautiful commemorative medal, a D-Day Normandy Map, a Remembrance Day poppy and COVID face mask to protect me from the hidden viral enemy. Stay thirsty my friends!

On March 18, 2021, exactly one year after the national health emergency was declared, I received my first dose of the AstraZeneca COVID vaccine at a local pharmacy. Mila and Mila received their vaccinations the following week. It was a seamless process, booking online to get on a waitlist and then getting an appointment scheduled shortly thereafter. Afterwards, we all breathed a great sigh of relief, knowing that we now had some protection from the deadly virus.

# Solitary Confinement

My father, who lives across the country in British Columbia, was feeling the effects of the COVID fatigue, being confined to his senior citizen's residence. During the early stages of the pandemic, the residents were confined to their rooms, with their daily meals delivered and left outside the doors of their individual units. Essential supplies such as medications and groceries had to be delivered to the main floor reception. Outdoor excursions to get a haircut or to meet close family members were not permitted. It was akin to a POW camp but with extremely polite prison guards.

After a few months, the total lockdown restrictions were eased but life did not exactly return to normal. There had been a change in management at the facility, with the effects being felt mainly with respect to the quality of the meals. Almost every dinner, without exception, that my father consumed could be described by using one adjective, 'crap.' When the server would inquire, "How was your meal Sir?", Dad would respond sarcastically, "You should be proud that you were not responsible for cooking this."

Although he had a decent laptop computer with internet access, Dad being almost 95 years young, did not have the savvy to use video conferencing applications such as Zoom. My niece eventually purchased a simple video console designed for use by 'older generation' adults. Mina and I would video call him every night, right after he had returned from his communal dinner. After the video call, I would challenge him to an online cribbage game, which helped him pass the time before he retired for the evening.

Just a few years ago, he enjoyed living independently in a downtown condo, with easy access across the street from shopping and dining. We would regularly play 'Words with Friends', an online scrabble game, which he really enjoyed until he discovered that I was using a 'scrabble cheat' website to look up the words that I was playing. Often, as the game neared the end, he would have a healthy lead, only to see it instantly evaporate when I played my final letters, with a huge point total, winning the game. Afterwards, he would go to bed, but could not get to sleep, with the stunning memory of defeat still etched in his brain. Fortunately, our nightly cribbage games have turned out to be much more evenly matched.

# Bob Trudeau's Myeloma Story

In September, 2020, I read an inspiring online article about Bob Trudeau, a runner from Kamloops, British Columbia. He is not only an executive member of the local myeloma support group, but also a very accomplished runner. At the time, he had organized his own 50-km run/walk in support of multiple myeloma. Understanding the nature of the disease, I was so impressed with Bob's distance goal, that I sent him an email to offer my support and congratulations on his successful accomplishment on his very first ultra distance. Bob sent me a reply which read:

"Hi Paul,

Thank you for reaching out to contact me. The 50-km was definitely an effort, as I only run three times a week on trails and usually only up to 15-km now. Prior to the myeloma I enjoyed longer runs and am in awe of people that regularly run ultras as I only ran marathons and then one 50-km. It was in Manning Park, with 2,200 metres of vertical and it was a fabulous run. I would be happy to take you on a short run around Kamloops if you make it here and show you some of our fabulous trails. I love meeting with other people with Myeloma to hear their stories and offer any help or experience I can, especially for those who are newly diagnosed. As the primary co-leader of our support group, I have been lucky enough to be that primary go-to person for new members. Having myeloma is quite the journey and so different for so many people. I hope your wife is doing well and responding favourably to her treatment. Take care."

Bob had been diagnosed with multiple myeloma in 2017 after experiencing significant body pain during a training run. Medical imaging indicated several spinal fractures, which is a common myeloma defining event. Despite the debilitating aspects of the disease, Bob did not abandon his active lifestyle. Bob's dedication and courage remains an inspiration to us all.

During the COVID-19 pandemic, Bob emphasized the importance of following the public health guidelines surrounding physical distancing and wearing a face mask. From my own experience, the health protocols became a daily ritual to ensure that Mina was protected from the virus. As the pandemic went through multiple surges, I could not believe the selfishness and irresponsibility of some people, including a few of our politicians.

# A State of Denial

Why do some people insist on turning the public health crisis into a political football? Perhaps they view the guidelines as an attack on their own personal freedoms. Well excuse me, but your personal freedom ends when it infringes on my wife's, and everyone's personal health and safety. People who claim that they have a medical reason not to wear a mask in public indoor settings should not get a free pass. They should be ticketed and then have the opportunity to prove it in court.

The pandemic has seen the anti-maskers and the anti-vaxxer movement emerge in full force with almost a religious fervour. I noticed several posters placed at strategic intersections around Toronto proclaiming, 'People Dropping Dead After Receiving COVID shot.' The poster also has a reference to a website called 'VaccineFromHell.com.'

On the website itself, there a preposterous claim that the vaccine will 'alter your DNA and make it programmable by something other than Me. You will have become a mixture of something else, an altered form of man and technology, and therefore not in My image any longer.' The sad truth is that a certain percentage of the population could be persuaded by such misinformation. We can only hope that when the next pandemic arrives, history lessons will be learned, and a more informed public will act in line with the common good. I just pray that humanity is not destined to repeat the mistakes of the past.

## How I Became a Myeloma Guru

To become a multiple myeloma guru, one first needs to understand what the disease is all about. Your medical team does not necessarily have the time to educate you. There is a wealth of information on multiple myeloma available at your fingertips on various internet websites. If you would like to get individual patient survivor stories as a source of information, there are plenty of inspirational books available in either paperback or e-book formats. Joining a local myeloma support group will also prove to be a valuable source of knowledge. You and your loved one can learn directly from first-hand accounts of other patients and caregivers.

I found the following websites to be extremely informative and useful. There is a wealth of educational material and webinars hosted by recognized doctors:

- Myeloma Canada (www.myelomacanada.ca)
- Multiple Myeloma Research Foundation-MMRF (www.themmrf.org)
- The International Myeloma Foundation (www.myeloma.org)
- Myeloma Crowd (www.myelomacrowd.org)

Some of the myeloma organizations offer downloadable applications which enable you to input your medical data, symptoms and drug treatment program. I preferred using my own hand-written journal which was more personalized compared with a digital format.

## Get a Basic Understanding of the Disease

Simply stated, multiple myeloma is a type of cancer that begins in the plasma cells. These are a type of white blood cell that develop in the bone marrow. They are an essential component of the body's immune system. Healthy plasma cells produce proteins that defend the body against attacks from viruses and bacteria.

When the genetic code (DNA) in the plasma cell gets corrupted, the cells multiply out of control. The plasma cells then crowd out all the healthy red and white blood cells in the bone marrow, resulting in a compromised immune system. The cancerous plasma cells secrete defective proteins into the blood and urine. This results in many serious consequences, as witnessed in my fictionalized stories from the mid-nineteenth century to 1947.

Dr. Reece advised us that the cause of multiple myeloma is unknown, as is the case with most cancers. However, if I had to hazard a guess, I suspect Mina's myeloma was a direct result of the radioactive iodine that she took to get rid of the residual thyroid cancer cells back in 2001. It does not take a medical expert to imagine a healthy plasma cell migrating from the bone marrow and then receiving a radiation dose from the iodine. The cell's DNA would become compromised before moving back to the bone marrow where it would transform into myeloma and rapidly proliferate. I would not be surprised if her low-grade oral cancer was also linked to the ingestion of the iodine tablets.

## Know Your Medical Specialists

Currently, there is no routine screening for multiple myeloma. Your family doctor may discover some anomalies through blood testing when you go for your annual physical. If you are extremely lucky, you then could be referred to a hematologist who could perform additional testing. This 'hit-or-miss' process sometimes enables detection of the disease at an early stage. More often than not, most myeloma patients get diagnosed when the disease is in the final stage, making treatment decisions much more challenging.

If there is a confirmation of multiple myeloma, it is essential to get seen by the right specialists. Your family doctor can be the primary contact who can act like a personal running coach, helping you navigate through the medical system with the various specialists. Since this disease tends to adversely affect a variety of functions, you and your loved one will be communicating with many different doctors who are all focused within their own areas. Your task will be to learn who does what and why. Sometimes this may involve cross-communicating with the specialists to ensure that everyone is working from the same script.

# Diagnostics and Monitoring

When Mina was first diagnosed, the doctors used a few key measures to make the call. These were the Lactate Dehydrogenase (LDH) and the Beta 2 Micro-Globulin blood tests. Also key to the diagnosis were the identification of the CRAB symptoms. The doctors will combine all of the diagnostic results and symptoms to determine the stage of the cancer. Learning about these tests and the international staging system in advance will allow you to become a more informed patient advocate.

The bone marrow biopsy is a routine diagnostic procedure that you should also research before it is done. I was extremely frustrated when the doctors could not get a viable sample from the bone marrow. They said that Mina's specific genetic mutation could not be determined since the marrow produced a 'dry tap.' If the patient advocate knows the myeloma genetic mutation, this could inform better treatment options to be discussed later with the medical team.

There are also a number of imaging studies that will be performed such as X-rays, MRI's and CT/PET scans. Each one of these techniques has advantages and disadvantages. Do not hesitate to ask your hematologist the purpose of the type of imaging scan being performed. They are mainly used to measure the amount of bone damage caused by the cancer. Some tests involve the use of tracing dyes which provide clarity but may come at a risk of kidney impairment.

Recall the following tests given to Mina to help make the correct diagnosis:

- Serum Protein Electrophoresis (SPEP)
- Urine Protein Electrophoresis (UPEP)
- Immunofixation Electrophoresis (IFE)
- Free Light Chain Assay

These are initially used for diagnostic purposes, and later for on-going monitoring to measure the effectiveness of treatment. There are plenty of online videos entitled 'Know Your Labs' that can help you develop a greater understanding of the purpose of these tests.

## Balance in Treatment Options

I have come to learn that every myeloma patient is unique in the sense that the disease has many different sub-types and risk levels. Your medical team will use genetic testing to determine if your loved one falls into the standard or the high-risk category. This combined with the diagnostic tests will determine the course of treatment.

If you do the basic research into the biology of the disease, you can become more informed as a patient advocate. This will allow you to become an active member when the hematologist discusses treatment options for your loved one.

For example, a high-risk patient will likely require a more aggressive treatment approach. If you are an informed patient advocate, you can respectfully disagree with the doctor's recommendation if you feel it would result in a poor quality of life for your loved one. The trick is to seek an option that will knock back the cancer while still ensuring a relatively good quality of life. It becomes all about balancing the costs and benefits of a specific therapy.

# Drug Names

Every drug has an approved generic or medical name, decided on by an expert committee. Many drugs are also known by a brand or trade name chosen by the pharmaceutical company making and selling that drug as a medicine. As an example of the drug naming convention, Lenalidomide, the medical name, is also known as Revlimid, the brand name.

Generic names for drugs are nowadays constructed out of affixes and stems that classify the drugs into different categories and also separate drugs within categories. For example, the drug Daratumumab, has the affix 'mab', which is an abbreviation of a category referring to this drug as a 'monoclonal antibody.'

At first, I found this naming convention to be confusing at best and annoying at worst. However, as a myeloma patient caregiver and advocate, I quickly learned the value of learning both the medical and brand names. More often than not, I would stumble over the pronunciation of the medical name, only to discover that the brand name would not be a formidable tongue twister.

The medical professionals to whom I conversed with also frequently switched back and forth between the two names. Learning the drug categories through the affix also took a bit of research and effort, but proved to be very informative. You want to become a semi-expert in the drug name-game if only for the sake of your loved one. After a while, the two-drug names become burned into one's brain and the recall will almost be second nature. Learning in advance the drug category will inform you of exactly how the drug is expected to work and the possible side-effects.

This is a process of self-education and is not unlike learning a foreign language. My experience with second language acquisition of Mandarin Chinese probably helped me navigate the drug naming maze. Believe me, the effort to de-code Chinese writing was much more

intense!

# Thalidomide : A Blessing in Disguise

The history of scientific progress is punctuated with novel drugs that were discovered by accident or by pure luck. Some drugs, originally invented for a specific purpose, later get re-purposed for effective treatment of other medical conditions. Thalidomide, which eventually became a key 'go-to' therapy in the treatment of multiple myeloma, was no exception.

There is a famous Chinese proverb 'Sai Weng Shi Ma' (塞翁失馬) which has the English equivalent of 'every dark cloud has a silver lining.' Sai Weng, was an old man living on the frontier where he raised horses. One day he lost one of his horses. When his neighbors comforted him, Sai Weng simply asked, "Who knows if this is a good thing or a bad thing?" After a while, the lost horse returned and with another beautiful horse. The neighbor came over again and congratulated Sai Weng on his good fortune. But Sai Weng simply asked again, "Who knows if this is a good thing or a bad thing?"

One day, his son went out for a ride with the new horse. He was violently thrown from the horse and broke his leg. The neighbors once again expressed their condolences. But Sai Weng repeated his question, "Who knows if this is a good thing or a bad thing?" One year later, the Emperor's army arrived at the village to recruit all able-bodied men to fight in the war. Because of his injury, Sai Weng's son could not go off to war, and was spared from certain death. The outcome was a blessing in disguise.

The story of thalidomide is one of tragedy followed by its remarkable success in fighting multiple myeloma. It was truly a blessing in disguise. Using the drug as a successful myeloma therapy was certainly the 'silver lining within the dark cloud', an unexpected consequence.

I propose to expand this idiom to say 'every myeloma plasma cell has a silver lining.' The bad news is that multiple myeloma causes an incredible amount of damage to the body through many different mechanisms. The good news is that myeloma plasma cells have an Achilles heel that can be targeted by novel drug therapies.

# Treatment Decisions : All Roads Lead to Rome

In Chinese, there is a famous idiom, 条条大路通罗马. The identical idiom can be found in English, meaning 'All roads lead to Rome.' The phrase refers to the use of different means to obtain the same result. You could also say, 'there is more than one way to skin the proverbial cat.'

Our hematologists at the Princess Margaret Cancer Centre explained to us that myeloma cancer cells are smart. The cancer can be put into a deep remission with initial treatments. However, after a period of time, new genetic mutations emerge that provide the cancer cell with a mechanism to resist and overcome existing drug therapies. The myeloma blood markers then slowly trend upwards, resulting in a progression of the disease and relapse. Alternative drug therapies must then be explored to get the cancer back under control.

But there is hope in addressing this issue. One does not have to stand by idly as Nero fiddles and Rome burns to the ground. If one exit door in the cancer cell is shut and a second door is opened, new drugs can slam the second door shut. As a patient caregiver, I learned that the choice of any drug therapy involves a team approach.

In making the right treatment decision for your loved one, the doctors will always recommend an option that balances quality of life with an effective therapy. I quickly learned that the myeloma drugs are not benign agents. They can be extremely potent and cause serious side effects. You as a patient caregiver and advocate will be tasked with the heavy responsibility of the daily monitoring of symptoms, either from the drugs or the cancer itself.

# Relapsed and Refractory Myeloma

As a patient caregiver and advocate, I found it useful to read peer-reviewed research articles that evaluated both the safety and effectiveness of both existing and new drug therapies. Although these articles tend to be quite technical in nature, they can be informative and offer hope that progress is steadily being made in developing a cure.

Sooner or later, hopefully later, the cancer will return (relapse). It may also become resistant or not respond to the existing drug maintenance therapy (refractory). There will be a need to discuss different treatment options with the hematologist. This is where your research into the science can make you an informed patient advocate.

The research will usually reference some common terms such as progression free survival, overall survival and hazard ratios. The results expressed in chart form may be confusing. There will be statistical tests included in the results to compare the treatment group with the placebo group. As you proceed with your self-education, the terms will become more familiar. Eventually, you may come to consider yourself a semi-expert in the subject matter. Congratulations, you have arrived!

The medical team will likely ask if you have heard of a specific drug that your loved one may benefit from if the current maintenance program needs to be tweaked. Having the advance knowledge of how a specific drug works and the potential side-effects will inform how both you, your loved one and the doctors will make the next treatment decision. Remember that it is always a team approach.

# Clinical Trials

As a multiple myeloma patient advocate, always be on the look-out for a clinical trial that might be appropriate for your loved one to participate in. A clinical trial could be a game-changer especially in the case of relapsed or refractory myeloma. I found this to be one of the most challenging, yet frustrating tasks. Do not expect the clinical drug trial to arrive at your doorstep neatly gift-wrapped. From my experience, the opportunity to take part in a clinical drug trial depends upon timing and a bit of luck.

Through clinical trials, doctors find new ways to improve treatments and the quality of life for people with disease. Any time you or a loved one needs treatment for cancer, clinical trials are an option to think about. Today, people are living longer lives from successful cancer treatments that are the results of past clinical trials.

In Canada, finding a suitable clinical trial for multiple myeloma patients tends to be quite challenging. One hematologist explained to us that 'all the stars and planets have to be perfectly aligned' in order for a patient to be considered for a clinical trial. The eligibility criteria for clinical trial participants are quite rigidly defined, for good reason. No matter how many obstacles that there are to negotiate, locating a clinical trial for your loved one must remain a top priority for the patient caregiver and advocate.

# Precision Medicine

With all of the newly-developed drug therapies to treat multiple myeloma, why is there such a variable response in the patient population? Some folks do extremely well, achieving a complete remission which continues for many years. The disease in other patients seems to be unresponsive to the drug therapies, resulting in worsening of the symptoms and eventual death within a short timeframe. I was extremely dismayed to learn from our hematologist that, no matter which treatment is chosen, the disease eventually returns and becomes resistant to the prior drug therapies.

The reason why a 'one-size-fits-all' approach to treatment results in inconsistent outcomes relates to the genetics of this disease. As in most cancers, there are many different genetic mutations or defects that determine the course of multiple myeloma. Some folks have standard-risk disease while others are classified as high-risk. Mina's diagnosis fell into the high-risk category.

Imagine a dam that develops a hole and springs a leak. We manage to plug that hole in the dam only to find that two new holes have opened up in another location. To make matters worse, the cement we used to plug the first hole is totally useless in stopping the leaks in the newly formed holes. We are now forced to invent a new type of cement to stop the dam from bursting. Failing that, we can look for a new strategy, such as finding the true source of the problem upstream.

Although Mina's exact sub-type of myeloma could not be determined, the doctors always gave us hope that it would be identified at some point in the future. Currently, there is a new procedure called 'Free Cell DNA' which is in clinical trials. Instead of using an invasive bone marrow biopsy, scientists are using blood serum to analyze the genetic changes occurring in the plasma cells found in the blood. Regardless of the whether the gene mutations are found by bone

marrow sampling or by blood serum testing, it would be only a matter of time before a novel

drug is invented that would be a precision-fit to target Mina's myeloma sub-type.

# The Swiss Cheese Model

The Swiss Cheese model of accident causation is a model used in many different fields, including healthcare. The model illustrates that, although many layers of defense lie between hazards and accidents, there are flaws in each layer that, if aligned, can allow the accident to occur.

This concept fits quite nicely with the approach to current drug therapies in multiple myeloma. In the Swiss cheese model, an organisation's defenses against failure are modeled as a series of barriers, represented as slices of cheese. The holes in the slices represent weaknesses in individual parts of the system and are continually varying in size and position across the slices. The system produces failures when a hole in each slice momentarily aligns, permitting an opportunity so that a hazard passes through holes in all of the slices, leading to a failure.

In terms of myeloma drug therapy, the multiple cheese slice layers represent all of the current lines of drug therapies we use to defend against the disease. Eventually, the drugs lose their ability to control the cancer when the holes in the cheese slices align. The 'accident' reflects the ability of a cancer cell to eventually overcome the effectiveness of many different drugs, leading to a return of active disease, known as relapse. However, scientists continue to discover new and innovative 'cheese slices' (drug therapies) as they race to find a cure for multiple myeloma.

# Precision Medicine for Runners

Precision medicine also has many applications in the world of running. Runners of all levels of ability will eventually encounter injuries that require attention and the right prescription. Such injuries usually are a result of over-training, inappropriate running shoes or poor biomechanics.

When I first started my running program back in the early nineties, I made the fatal error of choosing cross-training shoes for my running workouts. After logging multi-100-kilometre weeks of mileage, I soon developed a painful case of plantar fasciitis, which is an inflammation of the thick band of tissue extending along the bottom of the feet.

After visiting a local running store and speaking with the experts, I learned of the importance of investing in proper pair of running shoes. More important, the type of shoe selected has to match the biomechanics of the individual runner. There are three basic types of running shoes; neutral, stability and motion control. Since I tended to over-pronate, where the ankle and arch roll slightly inward, I needed stability running shoes. This precision prescription resolved my injury and I was soon back to pain-free running.

Near the final stretch of my first marathon in 1995, the tendon on my right leg was rubbing against my knee bone, causing an incredible amount of pain and discomfort. After the race, I paid a visit to a podiatrist who diagnosed my problem as iliotibial band syndrome. The IT band is a long piece of connective tissue that runs along the outside of the leg from the hip to the knee and shinbone. I had to get a custom-made orthotic shoe inserts to correct my running form. This precision solution solved my problem. I had no issues in any of my future running events.

Drugs have also played a role in running, both for legitimate and illegitimate purposes. Over-the-counter medicines such as aspirin or ibuprofen can help deal with muscle inflammation after an intense competition. I once had to get a cortisone shot from a sports medicine doctor to deal with intense knee inflammation prior to a 72-hour ultra running race. This allowed me to start the race but the injury quickly transferred to my hip, reducing me to a death march for the final two days of the race. The bottom-line is that the body is smart and adapts to almost any type of drug. On a micro level, cancer cells also adapt and eventually become resistant to therapy.

# 2037 : The London Marathon

It was a warm spring day for the start of the 2037 London marathon. Almost thirty-thousand runners lined up at the start on Charlton Road in southeast section of the city, in the south section of Greenwich Park. Among them was an eighty-year-old marathoner, the oldest in this year's race, who was attempting to break a marathon record for his age group.

He had been a runner for more than forty years and had just recently been able to reverse the age-related slowdown that inevitably happens with the advancement of years. New genetic editing techniques using CRISPR technology, by tweaking his mitochondrial DNA, gave his cardiovascular system the equivalent performance standard of a competitor half his age. He could now run at a steady seven minute per mile pace with relative ease, making a sub-three-hour marathon a realistic goal again. In fact, so many marathon runners had taken advantage of gene editing, the Boston Marathon had to impose much stricter qualification standards for all potential race entrants.

Just before the starting gun, the race director paid tribute to the elderly runner. His fellow competitors applauded him and then the race began. He was able to keep pace with the mid-pack runners, chatting with other runners as he ran with the three-hour pace bunny. Most of them were had not been born when he had run the 100th anniversary Boston Marathon back in 1996. They found it hard to believe that a three-hour marathon was the gold standard back then, while today it is considered to be just an average finish time.

The race continued east for three miles until turning north towards the Thames and then along Woolwich Road. At six miles, the course took the runners past the north section of Greenwich Park, where the famed observatory could be seen. At the half-way point in the race, runners crossed Tower Bridge and could view the infamous Tower of London on the north side of the Thames.

From there, the runners headed east again, looping back west after passing by Canary Wharf. Passing twenty-five miles, they ran by the Westminster Bridge and could see St. Thomas' Hospital on the other side of the Thames. This was the hospital that Dr. Solly treated his multiple myeloma patients, although the facility had since been relocated to Lambeth from Southwark. The runners were now less than one mile from the finish line of the marathon in St. James' Park.

Suddenly, the eighty-year-old marathoner slowed and stopped. Off to his left, he could see Westminster Abbey. He was captivated by the building. He removed his running cap and placed it over his heart, as if to pay tribute. A race official beckoned to him, "Sir, you are close to the finish line. Don't stop now. You can easily break three hours."

The runner replied, "My three-hour time goal is still intact. I just had to pay homage to the man who lies buried there. Humanity owes him a debt of gratitude. He built the foundations upon which our knowledge grew. We have evolved and still evolving." With those words, he continued with his final sprint toward the finish line, around Memorial Gardens, to finish on The Mall in St. James Park in a time of 2:59:59. Another Boston marathon qualifying time was in the books!

As he walked back to his hotel in central London, he pondered his life as an accomplished runner. He was grateful for the CRISPR genetic editing that extended his competitive running career. The technology was now being applied to the first human colonies on the planet Mars, allowing rapid adaptation to the harsher Martian environment by modifying the genetic codes that governed respiration and body temperature regulation. Who knows, one day he could be among a select few of privileged runners invited to participate in the first marathon on Mars.

More importantly, the gene editing techniques were now being used to develop exciting new curative therapies for multiple myeloma patients. Functional cures, where the disease is ever-present but not detectable, were developed over the past twenty years. However, an absolute cure was just over the horizon. The year of the silver bullet was fast approaching.

# 2056 : Year of the Silver Bullet

The year is 2056. Mina and I have already departed this life which means that this chapter was written in anticipation of future events. This year, another world record was set for the marathon, with Absko Otieno of Kenya breaking the previously unthinkable sub-two-hour standard for 26.2 miles, in a jaw-dropping time of 1:56:56 in the men's race of the London Marathon. The women's marathon race in Berlin was equally impressive with Magdala Girma of Ethiopia smashing the women's marathon world record with a time of 2:04:59. These previously unthinkable running performances were made possible through a combination of advanced scientific training methods and gene-editing techniques that selected for biological traits which optimized an individual's biomechanics and physiology.

Humans were not only controlling their own evolution but also tweaking their DNA to thwart disease and extend lifespans to an average of 130 years. Colonies on Mars have now been established for more than 10 years. Terraforming of the Martian planet was progressing at a rapid pace. Simple forms of ancient terrestrial life had already been discovered on Mars and were determined to be the pre-cursors of life on Earth. Nano-technology has enabled the launch of micro space probes to distant solar systems to search for habitable planets using quantum-photon propulsion, enabling spacecraft travel approaching the speed of light.

Multiple myeloma and every other form of cancer have been eradicated. Treatments for multiple myeloma, such as stem cell transplants, CAR-T cell therapy and monoclonal antibodies, previously considered to be 'innovative' and 'game-changing' were now viewed historically as very crude, almost medieval approaches to medicine. The problem with medicine in the 2020s stemmed from the objective of treating the symptoms of the disease rather than the underlying root genetic causes.

The shot-gun method using high-dose chemo drugs or even specially developed humanized antibodies were successful at slowing the pace of multiple myeloma, but did very little to halt the disease in its tracks. Relapse was always a foregone conclusion since the core genetic machinery in the heart of the cancerous plasma cell remained unaltered and left free to impose its destructive will as it evolved to become resistant to shot-gun therapy. Scientists could only play whack-a-mole with the disease for so long, until a silver bullet was developed in 2056. The cure came about as a result of exponential advances in the mRNA technology developed during the COVID-19 pandemic, precision medicine, DNA repair and manipulation, combined with the merging of quantum physics and medical research.

Specifically, the results of the International Myeloma Foundation's Black Swan research initiative (BSRI) which studied the entire population of Iceland over many decades, ultimately determined the hereditary and environmental factors underling the disease. It was determined that people who developed MGUS and then progressed on to active myeloma had a unique genomic feature called 'fractured genetics.'

Some folks, solely through the randomness of Darwin's process of natural selection develop a propensity for gene fragility. These are strictly defined segments of their DNA that were susceptible to becoming corrupted through mutational agents. Random genetic mutations are essential for human evolution and adaptation to ensure the overall survival of the species. Unfortunately, individual members of the species become collateral damage in the process.

Ionizing radiation from various sources was the key culprit in the development of fractured genetics in susceptible individuals. Travel at high altitudes by airplane with repeated radiation exposure is a causal factor. Tracer radiation used in various medical imaging techniques and the use of radioactive iodine were determined to be significant risk factors. The environmental agents that promoted the mutations also included several types of viruses, including Hepatitis C and HPV. There was also a very strong correlation with chemical agents used in the agricultural and petroleum industries.

The first ingredient of the silver bullet was CRISPR technology, a genome editing procedure, where significant advancements were made since research started in this area in 2014. The CRISPR genome editing technique resulted in the 2020 Nobel Prize in Chemistry being awarded to Emmanuelle Charpentier and Jennifer Doudna. Genome editing (also called gene editing). It is a group of technologies that give scientists the ability to change an organism's DNA.

These technologies allow genetic material to be added, removed, or altered at particular locations in the genome. CRISPR is short-form for 'clustered regularly interspaced short palindromic repeats.' CRISPR was adapted from a naturally occurring genome editing system in bacteria. The bacteria capture snippets of DNA from invading viruses and use them to create DNA segments known as CRISPR arrays. The CRISPR arrays allow the bacteria to 'remember' the viruses (or closely related ones). If the viruses attack again, the bacteria produce RNA segments from the CRISPR arrays to target the viruses' DNA. The bacteria then use an enzyme to cut the DNA apart, which disables the virus.

By the year 2056, CRISPR technology had advanced to the point where scientists could precisely target genetic mutations in multiple myeloma plasma cells and then develop 'smart' programs to edit repairs directly within the cell nucleus. Merging CRISPR technology with the mRNA nano particle proved to be another key innovation.

The second component of this game-changing technology centers around the advancements in artificial intelligence (AI) and quantum computing. Oncology AI projects received a huge boost in public funding. Private companies including IBM, Alphabet and Amazon merged their AI resources to develop an AI oncology product that became the 'brains' behind the delivery system. Instead of just making cancer treatment decisions, AI evolved into making cancer cure decisions.

Powerful quantum computers were finally developed. The novel computing technology played a key role in analyzing the 3 billion bits of genetic information contained in the human genome, the product of the human genome project completed in the late 1980s. Scientists were able to decode this massive amount of data and understand the function of every single gene in the human DNA. More importantly, worldwide population genetic studies in gene mutations provided scientists the predictive power to determine the risks for specific gene defects and then implement therapeutic strategies for curing just about every type of disease.

The third component of the silver bullet involved the development of specialized nanobots. Researchers created nanobots in 2018 which were programmed to shrink cancer tumors by obstructing their blood supply. Since 2018, research in this area advanced by leaps and bounds. The cancer-seeking nanobots were eventually equipped with the artificial intelligence (AI) that enabled them to learn to recognize all of the permutations and combinations involved in plasma cell DNA mutations. Nanobots became the delivery vehicle that carried the CRISPR technology to its final destination.

Unlike present-day CAR-T cells, the nanobots, by nature of their design, are never capable of becoming exhausted. Once infused, they work 24/7, for a lifetime, going after defective plasma cells, delivering a CRISPR DNA repair mechanism directly to the cell's nucleus. The plasma cells are not destroyed, but rather repaired, which enables them to produce normal immunoglobulins. The cells are then able to self-destruct through normal apoptosis (cell death). It does not matter that there are an average of 12,000 genetic mutations experienced by the typical multiple myeloma patient through the course of the disease. The new technology effectively recognizes and repairs them all.

The final component of the silver bullet was the development of a quantum energy source to provide never-ending power for the nanobots. Many of the innovations associated with the development of quantum computing were incorporated in the design. For the quantum design to work properly, three entangled photons were fused with the new molecule.

The result was faster-than-light speed drug delivery and processing. The photons are replenished by a miniaturized laser within the nanobot. The quantum molecules are also capable of being in two locations at the same time, effecting DNA repairs rapidly and efficiently. It does not matter if a genetic mutation is a translocation, deletion or an augmentation, the molecule will target the key oncogenes, determine the defect, snip it using CRISPR and then repair and return the DNA to a normal state. It can also turn specific genes on or off, which means that tumour suppressor genes that were turned off through mutations can now be re-activated by CRISPR technology.

The new molecule has the drug affix 'QEM' attached to its name. The 'QEM' is an acronym for 'Quantum Entangled Molecule.' A one-time infusion in early adulthood provides a lifetime of protection from cancer. The QEM vaccine represents both a prevention and a cure. However, the monitoring of results cannot be done. As it is the norm for quantum physics, any attempt to observe the results will change the outcome. The effects of the quantum therapy would disappear after any attempt to measure it. A Chinese medical researcher and an American physicist shared the Nobel prize in medicine and physics respectively for the discovery.

Over the past 100 years multiple myeloma had claimed the lives of more than 10 million people world-wide. The economic and social burden of the disease was extreme. It took an investment of hundreds of trillions of dollars in medical research to provide a cure in 2056. With the development of the QEM silver bullet, this nightmare is finally over.

## Epilogue

If there is one consistent theme expressed in this book, it would be that of evolution. I don't mean this strictly in the sense of the biological processes found in Darwinian evolution. Rather, we witness an evolution of historical milestones related to multiple myeloma.

The science behind cancer research is an evolutionary process. We witness early medical researchers observe the biology of myeloma plasma cells and the impact on human health. They may make educated guesses based on the limitations of the technology available to them at a given point in time. Sometimes they are partially correct in their assumptions and often they are totally wrong. But science tends to be a self-correcting in that it leads itself open to critical review by peers who then revise the theoretical foundations, paving the way for new discoveries.

Drug therapies follow a similar evolutionary path, from seemingly preposterous rhubarb infusion treatments of the past all the way to present-day monoclonal antibodies. Trial and error approaches to drug treatments gave way to the evolution of the scientific method of modern-day clinical trails.

More significantly, there has been a transition towards achieving a cure for multiple myeloma. This objective is not outside the realm of probability. All of the elements in the preceding chapter outlining the 'silver bullet' currently exist within separate, yet interconnected scientific domains. Sooner or later, these will become integrated in theory, thought and action. It is just a matter of time.

Within the world of statistics and probability, there is a concept called the infinite monkey theorem. It states that a monkey hitting keys at random on a typewriter keyboard for an infinite amount of time will almost surely type any given text, such as the complete works of William Shakespeare. However, the probability that monkeys filling the entire observable universe would type a single complete work, such as Shakespeare's Hamlet, is so tiny that the chance of it occurring during a period of time hundreds of thousands of orders of magnitude longer than the age of the universe is extremely low. There is simply not enough space-time in the Einsteinian universe for this to become a reality.

The cure for multiple myeloma will not be the product of a statistically improbable mathematical equation. Do you really believe that a monkey typing for all eternity will eventually produce a clinical cure for multiple myeloma? There is no complex formula that is a substitute for human imagination and creativity.

Scientists create theories, some based on hunches and others based on valid empirical observations. Sometimes they write research papers on cancer that are total speculation, with the results being further challenged by new research. Many years down the road, theories either get discarded or refined. We see the art of creative thinking mixed with rational clinical studies. Often there is an element of pure luck where a researcher stumbles upon a discovery. Sometimes a researcher's efforts get dismissed, only to become validated many years later. The contribution to the myeloma knowledge base has a cumulative impact over time. Anything that can be imagined will ultimately happen, including a cure. Monkeys need not apply.

The bottom-line is that there has been very slow progress in the treatment of multiple myeloma over the past 100 years. However, the development of new and innovative treatment options has dramatically extended overall survival rates. It is similar to an elite marathon runner who starts out at a very slow pace and then rapidly accelerates in the final 5 kilometres to the finish line. The cure finish line is coming into sight.

The same concepts apply in the world of running. Runners use a technique called creative visualization, a psychological tool, to maximize performance, be it in a race or a training regimen. Sometimes, a specific goal seems to be totally unachievable, whether it is a personal best performance or winning a race outright.

Eventually, through a sustained effort, all training components seem to come together to produce an unexpected result. A runner will imagine breaking the three-hour barrier in a marathon or finally besting a rival competitor in a race. This does not happen by accident or by pure luck. A training program in running is similar to the steady progress made by myeloma cancer researchers. Individual components of the program build upon each other, just as a scientific knowledge base is built through experimentation, repetition and hard work. But the initial impetus is human imagination which is the spark that results in a successful outcome or cure.

As a dedicated myeloma patient caregiver, you will also go through an evolution. At first, there is a sense of bewilderment. It is a disease that not very many people, including family doctors, are familiar with. There is a struggle to make sense of the symptoms, diagnosis, treatment options, combined with an unclear prognosis. Next, you will find the medical terminology confounding. Eventually, a tiny bit of research and self-education will make the murky waters easier to navigate.

You will then proceed through the process of 'team-building' that involves the formation of a social support network which includes medical specialists, immediate family, myeloma support groups and friends. You will become a semi-expert in the subject matter, with the ability to advocate on behalf of your loved one, the best course of action. The final phase involves the development of a treatment strategy in consultation with your medical team. Unlike a marathon race, there seems to be no finish line in sight, only an endless series of detours.

If you manage to keep your sanity, the road ahead will become less rocky. If you are lucky, you will have come to realize a purposeful mission in your life. That mission will involve the provision of unconditional care and support for your loved one. After all, what nobler cause could there be for someone for whom you have pledged to stand by in sickness and in health, right from the very beginning?

Made in the USA
Monee, IL
03 July 2021

72841018R00138